The

Red

Claw

Book 1 of the Sea Purrtector Files

Copyright 2014 by Jeanne Foguth

Cataloging-in-Publication Data is on file with the Library of Congress.

Paperback ISBN: 978-0-9913338-6-8

Acknowledgements, Etc.:

For years, our family had the privilege of being owned b y Rahma, alias Rom or Rahm. Whatever we called him, we thought he was the best cat in the world for the sixteen wonderful years he owned us. And since his passing, have not found any reason to change that opinion.

I have been thinking about writing a novel from a cat's perspective as a tribute to Rahma and believe that Xander de Hunter does Rom justice.

~

Many thanks to my faithful beta and proof readers, without whom my work would have 'rogue commas' and 'renegade spelling' and all sorts of strange anomalies. Thank you, Kensleigh, Justin, Victoria, Paul, Kaj, P.J. and Pauline Nicolai, who are great gremlin-hunters. I don't know what I would do without you grammar-nazis.

Thank you also to Kiara Graham for her prowess with digital design, and work on The Red Claw's cover.

The Red Claw 1

Chapter 1

Xander supervised his humans, Mike and Ginny de Hunter, as their dingy circumnavigated Flamingo Cay, a lifeless piece of Bahamian rock, which wasn't home to any birds, let alone something as exotic as a flamingo.

As they rounded the last dark, rugged point of dead rock, Xander noticed a familiar cabin-cruiser lashed to Whispurring Winds, his immaculate sailboat. Whiskers bristling with irritation at having the filthy boat and it's stupid, braZen dog anywhere near him, Xander stared in disbelief. A moment later, Mike's eyes bulged and he increased the dinghy's speed. "I can't believe they had the audacity to tie their boat to ours."

Ginny looked forward, shading her eyes from the harsh mid-day sun. "Is that C Pause?"

"Do you know of any other red cabin-cruiser?"

Ginny glared at Mike, "It's your own fault." He stared at her as if she'd grown gills. "Weeks ago, back when we were anchored at Allen Cay, you told Nan and Jim to 'hook up to us' if they 'happened across us'."

"But I didn't mean that literally." Mike gestured to C Pause. "They didn't even bother putting down an anchor – just tied onto our stanchions! What kind of an idiot does that?"

The kind with a dumb dog for a mascot, Xander thought.

Mike's face turned an odd shade of red that neither sun nor wind could duplicate. If the turquoise water hadn't been home to jelly fish, sharks and barracuda, Xander would have leaped over the dinghy's fat round sides and swum to Whispurring Winds to make certain that Valentine, the vile dog, who lived on C Pause wasn't snooping in his things.

"Its probably safer to have them tied to us." Ginny wrinkled her nose. "Back at Allen, they never set their anchor well and I'd rather not have them drag into us, if the wind picks up."

Xander studied C Pause. The only difference in its appearance seemed to be that there were more fat bags of trash tied to its rails. Since the breeze was at his back, he couldn't tell – yet – if the stink had improved, but he doubted it. The nasty red motorboat had been infested with all sorts of dreadful things, the worst being the dog who lived aboard.

As soon as he got back on board, he checked everything, but nothing seemed to have been tampered with. Still, there was a dog's boat tied to his starboard side, so precautions were wise. As covertly as possible, Xander armed several of his sensors to monitor C Pause.

Hours later, as Xander wrote his report for the Catamondo Council about Flamingo Key, a starboard line groaned and a warning light began to blink, Xander flicked a paw over his keyboard bringing up his purrsonal security grid. The camera on top of Whispurring Winds' mast showed wilted sails and moonlight glistening off the glass smooth surface of the Caribbean Sea, which meant an intruder had crept aboard from C Pause. A second sensor on the starboard side began to blink.

Xander knew who the spy was and that, even if the more obvious cameras didn't show him in the shadows, he was there and moving. Shivers ran up and down his spine as his paws became a blur while he concealed his surveillance program and the Top Secret Document he'd been working on. Paws flying, he encode his cypher; instantly Catamondo's security files became invisible.

For several moments, the only sounds he heard were the typical ones his humans made during a calm night: Mike's soft snores and the quiet rustle when Ginny turned a page. Then came a muffled movement above deck accompanied by a tiny list to starboard.

The prowler was not fully aboard on the forward deck.

Xander's tail twitched with anger.

Stealthy sounds indicated that the mutt was heading toward the starboard porthole, which offered a view of the interior of his cabin.

While his acute hearing monitored each tiny, furtive movement, Xander finished concealing his files. Ears perked, he clicked on the screensaver. Irritation mixed with anticipation at the mind games he could play with the dumb dog.

He glanced up at the cockpit, noted Ginny's unresponsiveness to the dog's presence and made a mental note to work on her training. Before Valentine was close enough to peer into his cabin, Xander leaped to a cushion in the salon and sprawled across its emerald fabric. By force of will, he relaxed his muscles, laid his head on his paws and closed his eyes. Several heartbeats later, webbing sighed as Valentine's snotty nose pressed against the porthole's screen. Xander counted to ten, then pretended to wake up and groggily look around Whispurring Winds' salon. He feigned surprised when he noticed the boxer's nose squashed against the mesh. "What are you doing here?" Xander sat up as if stiff with sleep.

Valentine's drippy tongue lolled over his horrible pointy teeth. "You doing okay?"

"Until you woke me," Xander snapped. He stretched so he could glimpse the clock. Unless Ginny stayed stuck in her novel, his humans would change watch soon, so time was limited.

"It's scary tonight," Valentine whined, his baggy skin quivering like Jell-O. "I can hear stuff moving out there, but I can't see anything."

"Look for flying fish on the decks in the morning." Xander yawned hoping he could convince the dog that he was a very shallow, sleepy cat. "They're kinda bony, but if you get to the over-nighters early enough, they're fresh." His tail slashed in irritation when he realized he was giving the pesky boxer useful advice.

"So that's why you go out on deck so early every morning." The wrinkles deepened until the fangs were visible. "I've always wondered."

As he suspected the dumb dog had been watching his activities. "Well, now you know." The question was if Valentine actually had not understood his above-board routine or if he was simply using that as a lame excuse to pry. Too bad the dog had been so intrigued that he'd motivated his humans to hear an invitation in Mike's careless words.

Xander yawned and stretched. Things were awfully dull at the moment and he was nearly done analyzing the Bahamian Islands for potential feline sanctuaries, so confusing the snoopy dog might be fun. Valentine shifted and a wave of putrid-dog-odor assailed Xander's nose. "When was the last time your humans bathed you?" He gave a slight shudder, thankful that his elegant seal point coat had never smelled so vile. No matter how boring things were, he wasn't desperate enough to deal with that stench. The sooner the sun rose, the sooner the boats would be free of each other and the sooner Valentine would be confined to C Pause's filthy decks.

"Bathe?" Valentine said, as if he didn't know the meaning of the word. He looked over his back, then huddled closer to the open porthole, as if he expected the lifelines to flip him over the side for a much-needed soaking. "How long will these doldrums last?"

Obviously the annoying dog had been rolling in his own excrement, again. It was all Xander could do not to take a step backward. "Only Hathor knows the weather. You really should get your humans to give you a bath, you'll feel much better." And so will my stomach, he added silently.

Valentine stared at him as if he'd sprouted a second head. If the mutt had been another cat he would have given him detailed hygienic advice, but most dogs seemed incapable of good grooming. And if this one didn't even know the definition of 'bath'.... To break his train of thought, Xander yawned, again. "Why did you come aboard my ship without permission?" In the ensuing moments, while he waited for an answer, the only sound was Mike's soft snores.

"I hope the sun drives away the fog tomorrow."

Fog? What fog he wondered. If it hadn't been for Ginny not wanting Mike to hurt Nan and Jim Danvers' feelings, he wouldn't have a stinky dog leaning against his screen or be wasting his valuable time acting like he didn't have anything better to do than discuss the weather with an imbecile, who was either too dumb to distinguish between nighttime and mist or too dumb to think up a more clever comment.

Or else the beast was trying to make him think he was stupid.

He'd supposedly just woken up, so how would he know the night was clear? "That would be nice." Xander glanced toward the cockpit, where Ginny was engrossed in her book. He'd deal with her later, for now he needed to play the part of an imbecile. "Nights seem shorter when I sleep through them." Xander gave such a big yawn his jaw hurt.

Another wrinkle appeared on Valentine's furrowed forehead. "I never noticed."

Pretending fatigue, he allowed his body to slump. "You should go home, find your cozy spot and relax," he urged, "you'll feel better by morning, but don't sleep late or the over-nighters won't be fresh."

Valentine smiled. "Thanks, buddy, I'll do that." Amazingly, he disappeared into the night.

Xander plopped onto the cushion, continuing his charade of exhaustion. The mutt landed on his own boat, then his claws clattered across C Pause's fiberglass deck. Xander's tail slapped the emerald fabric with a vengeance. The utter gall of that creature! How dare he act like they were friends! How dare he come aboard Whispurring Winds without an invitation! How dare he use the lame excuse of making sure he was all right as a cover for spying!

Xander froze and reviewed his thoughts.

What if the dogs suspected who he was? What if Valentine had been sent to spy on him? Obviously, the dog had been watching his above-board routine, but that would not have revealed anything, so there had to be some other reason why the dumb dog had felt the need to investigate further.

Had the mutt been sent to gather data on Catamondo's worldwide communication network?

Did the dogs know he'd been appointed The Sea Purrtector?

Did they know that he was responsible for organizing a program that would enable all seafaring cats access to their e-mail over boat radios?

Did the dogs suspect Catamondo was creating a worldwide system of safe places for abused and displaced cats?

Whatever he'd hoped to learn, the mutt would not find out anything from him. Xander padded up Whispurring Wind's steps, entered the cockpit and glared at Ginny, whose attention was supposed to alternate between her book and the cockpit monitor, but seemed to stay on the pages of the book. He could understand her neglect, since the monitor didn't have music, a story line or anything interesting enough to warrant the attention it got, but Mike always insisted that the boring thing needed to be constantly watched. Except it wasn't even good enough to keep an eye on C Pause.

He gave his humans high points for understanding that the situation with C Pause needed watching, but Ginny had lost points by first tolerating C Pause's arrival, and most recently by not noticing when Valentine came aboard.

Tomorrow, he would work on her training, but for now he had other things to do. Xander moved into the shadows, pausing for his eyes to adjust. Then, on paws soft as the night, he made a perimeter patrol of Whispurring Winds' deck, concentrating on the areas where Valentine had been. Aside from four blobs of slobber and some reddish hairs, it didn't look like the annoying animal had left anything behind. Xander returned to the cockpit. Whiskers twitching, he again studied the strange little screen his humans took such interest in. So what if the thing supposedly showed where Whispurring Winds was? So what if it could tell if there was a fish underneath their boat? Anyone could learn that simply by looking around. The screen was not all that accurate, either; when Xander had checked it at their anchorage in Stocking Cay's tidy-bowl-blue harbor, it had claimed their boat was in the middle of rock.

Xander snorted at the memory, then tail twitching with indignation, he padded back below to his laptop. He listened for several minutes before he sat down and tapped the space bar on the laptop; he didn't have enough time to finish the report, about Flamingo Cay only being acceptable as a temporary way-point for desperate cats fleeing from hurricanes, dogs or other atrocities.

But he had enough time to check his e-mail.

The longer it took the HAMM e-meter to transmit his

request, the faster Xander's tail twitched. Perhaps the satellite link was jammed or there was a bug in the program. Due to the amount of time he'd lost because of the nosy dog, he didn't have time to look for a problem in the software let alone deal with it.

The circle on the monitor lazily revolved, oblivious of his limited time and mounting frustration.

Finally, his e-mail scrolled onto the laptop. The first three were from Fluffy. Whiskers twirling with anticipation, he glanced at the clock; in twelve minutes the alarm would ding and his people would change shift. If he'd convinced the dog he was a dumb cat and unworthy of further surveillance, it had been time well spent.

Three red slashes flashed next to the eighth message. The Red Claw of Catamondo! The fur along Xander's spine stood up at the sight, which signified that something horrible had occurred. Xander glanced around the shadowed salon. Nothing stirred. He peered through the Plexiglas into the cockpit in time to see Ginny turn another page. If the story was that good, she might not wake Mike on time, regardless, he'd have time to hide his mail and feign slumber, so the worst that could happen would either be another rant about fur not belonging on the keyboard or cats not belonging on the desk.

He flicked the message open.

Kamikaze Xander, the message began. He scrolled to the signature at the bottom: Lady Mitzy Montgomery. His whiskers stiffened so violently he feared they'd leap off his face. Dear Hathor, why was the Purrsident writing to him? And why had she embedded The Red Claw of Catamondo on the message? Mouth dry, he started at the beginning.

My Dear Kamikaze Xander,
I hope you will purrsonally
investigate a situation, which is
near and dear to my heart. My
littermate, Dame Esmeralda,
has been catnapped. I fear the worst
and dare not trust this catastrophe
to anyone but the best.
That is you, my dear fellow.

Xander's spine snapped to attention.

Against my advice, Essy and her
human moved to Kingston, Jamaica
three years ago. I warned her that
the area had a bad reputation,
but Essy would not listen. She should
have. Last month, her human died
under mysterious circumstances and
now this. I digress, you need facts,
not emotion. I am attaching:
Essy's file
The initial note I received from Sir
Simon Morgan regarding the catnapping

Also, the file on Sir Simon, Purrtector of
   Jamaica

While I'm sure he wouldn't have been

voted into office if he were not qualified,

I know nothing of Sir Simon, since his file

is lacking. I do know you, and pray

to Hathor that you will be able

to purrsonally handle this horrible problem.

Sincerely, Lady Mitzy Montgomery

When he finished reading, Xander hopped onto the salon's cushion and clawed the green fabric until it began to pill. Frustration somewhat salved, he went back to the computer and reread the message: 'purrsonally investigate a situation'; 'purrsonally handle this horrible problem'. Hathor! How could he purrsonally do anything when one of Dogdum's spies was watching him so closely that their boats were tied together?

Was Valentine's arrival a coincidence or was he smarter than he appeared?

If Dogdum was involved in the vile catnapping and they guessed who he was, then it was certainly a telling coincidence that C Pause had tied up to Whispurring Winds mere hours before the crime.

He took a deep breath and acknowledged that it was a compliment for Lady M. to put such faith in him, but how could he coordinate a rescue effort when he wasn't familiar with the area, much less within a hundred nautical miles of Jamaica? Doubts aside, he needed to acknowledge the appeal, so he wrote:

My dear Lady Mitzy Montgomery,

He winced at how pompous it sounded, erased the screen and wrote Dear Lady Mitzy. No, no, no now it sounded too familiar. Dear Lady Montgomery, Yes, that sounded good. He continued:

Though I am hundreds of miles away, I shall

proceed to Jamaica immediately. Finding your beloved littermate will be my top priority.

Faithfully yours, Xander de Hunter

All Purrtectors were required to post their itinerary online and this wasn't the first time someone had not understood that a trip that normally took a car an hour or two, took at least a day by boat.

How could he coordinate anything from the middle of the doldrums? If C Pause stayed tied to them and Valentine continued to spy, it would be even more difficult to organize a rescue. Worse, if the wind did not return, he'd have to motivate his humans to fire up the noisy, smelly diesel engine that got even worse speed than the sails. His tail slapped the plotter so hard that Ginny put aside her novel and looked at the monitor. Xander quickly hid his mail program and closed the lid.

By the time Ginny came down to wake Mike, Xander was

curled on top of the fabric he'd shredded in his fit of frustration. When she passed him without caressing his ears, he knew he'd given a convincing performance of being asleep. Despite the rapid thudding of his heart, his whiskers twitched with pleasure.

Xander continued playing 'possum while his humans settled back into their normal nocturnal inactivity. Despite the fact that he barely moved a muscle, his mind was swirling around the red claw situation and what part he could play.

Perhaps the Jamaican Purrtector, Sir Simon, had merely told the Purrsident about the situation because she was Dame Esmeralda's sibling.

Perhaps Sir Simon didn't need or want help with his investigation.

And perhaps catnip grew on Mars.

Xander put his paw over his eyes. Sir Simon must have asked for help because he could not solve the abduction. He needed to stop the denial phase and accept the fact that he needed to find a way to resolve the mess. His fur quivered. Since moving aboard, 'somehows' always involved a nasty, wet dingy ride, which left his fur tasting of salt for days. Xander shivered at the memory of a recent dunking and the resulting fur-ball he had nearly gagged on.

Or perhaps Sir Simon had asked for help so he wouldn't be responsible for such a high profile case, which suggested the tom expected a bad outcome ... Xander feared this could end up being the fur-ball of all fur-balls.

Xander's hiss was drowned out by a soft rumbling sound. Cautiously raising one of his eyelids, he peaked under his paw, slowly, he turned his head until he could see into the cockpit. Mick sprawled in the white leather captain's seat, his jaw slack. After another snore, Xander moved into the cockpit on paws silent as the hidden moon. Standing behind the captain's seat, he made a visual search for Valentine, then, when nothing was seen, he conducted a security patrol of the deck, peeking into the hatches, he checked Whispurring Wind's interior. Though Ginny still clutched the novel, her eyes were closed, telltale crescents underneath her eyes testified to the fact that this was day four of anchoring in this desolate area with its rumors of drug smugglers and pirates. Since she obviously felt insecure here, it would be easy to get her to decide to go to Jamaica.

Without wasting another moment, Xander scooted back to the computer, opened his database and checked its encrypted files for Sir Simon's credentials. He didn't know what he'd expected the Chief Purrtector of Jamaica to be; a jaguar, perhaps. Whatever he'd expected, he hadn't imagined that any Maine Coons lived in the tropics, let alone got voted into a tropical island's highest office. Xander frowned, wondering why he'd never heard of Sir Simon. If the tom had risen through the ranks via the typical route – kickboxing tournaments – he should have heard of him after he won his first contest. He remembered a gnarly, scrappy tom named Scalpy from Jamaica who'd won the Caribbean Open two years previously. Scalpy had been a ruthless opponent, but he certainly hadn't been a Maine Coon.

Xander's frown deepened as he studied Sir Simon's handsome face. A tickle of worry shimmered at the edge of his thoughts, growing stronger as he thought about how voters in Los Angeles tended to vote for either well-known stars or pretty faces. His tail swished to dismiss the errant thought. Not all longhaired toms were sissies; his best pal, Merlin, an elegant white Norwegian Forest Cat with leaf-green eyes, looked movie-star handsome, but fought like a ninja, rode the waves like a surfer and cussed like a sailor.

They'd met when Merlin had insisted on accompanying him during an Emerald City investigation; Merlin had claimed that he could help find his missing sister because he knew her habits. Xander had been certain the pretty boy would hang around only as long as the ladies watched them from the shrubbery, then make up an excuse to back out. But the tom had been serious about locating his sister, and hadn't batted a whisker when the clues led them through the moonlight toward a dock, which was more dry rot than wood.

In fact, the only strange thing Merlin had done was grab a kite before he ran onto the dilapidated dock. Without thinking, he'd chased him. A leap before he caught him, the dock collapsed into the pounding waves. Merlin's whoop of unbridled glee had drowned out his own screech of panic. He'd swallowed his weight in water before he managed to fight his way back to the surface. Eyes stinging with the salt, he glimpsed Merlin laughing above the white froth. Then, the frigid talons had sucked down into the cold darkness, again.

He lost consciousness.

Awareness returned when he landed stomach first on something hard. Initially, he was certain fate had thrown him into the Styx, river of the dead, then, he'd heard another of Merlin's whoops of delight and opened an eye to see a white specter standing on his hind legs, head tilted back to laugh at the heavens. It took several blinks to recognize Merlin because his fur was so saturated that he appeared half his normal size. Xander hadn't been that wet since birth, an experience he felt fortunate not to recall. He had never been at eye level with whitecaps before, and couldn't quite figure out if he was alive or dead. Worse, he couldn't understand how he'd gotten onto a piece of broken plank or why the dock seemed to be getting farther and farther away.

Again, Merlin whooped with glee.

The tom was obviously demented and it was his bad luck not to have noticed the defect before he'd followed him onto that rotten dock. Now, they were balanced on flotsam and within a whisker of death.

"Hathor but I love water!" Merlin said.

The tom was definitely insane. "Are we dead?"

"Nope, just having fun!"

Mad beyond any doubt. "We're getting farther from shore."

"Cool, huh?" Merlin looked down, catching his look. "Can't you swim?"

"Of course not." He'd never imagined hearing such a ridiculous question.

"Oh, then you'd better hold on tight so I don't have to fish you out, again." Speechless, Xander stared at the tom, who had apparently saved him from the clutches of water, and didn't seem to realize how imperative it was for them to get back to land. Merlin somehow guided that rotten piece of wood out into the Puget Sound to where Cha-Cha clung to a drifting dinghy. She started yeowling when she recognized them moving toward her. As they came close, Merlin said, "How many times have I told you not to sharpen your claws on painters?"

"I only sharpen them on old rope," the indignant white Norwegian Forest Cat with the sun-burned nose retorted.

"What do you think a painter is?" Merlin meowed in exasperation. "The only dumber thing to do was go to sleep in the boat after you weakened the line."

"Whatever," she said. "Is that tom with you alive?"

"No," Xander responded, "I've passed on to live in my nightmares."

Cha-Cha's laugh skipped over the waves. The whole litter was crazy!

"Cut the chit-chat," Merlin ordered, "and hop aboard. We need to get back to shore while it's still too dark for any humans to see us." And amazingly, the tom had piloted that rotten plank right back to where they'd fallen in.

Xander shook his head at the memory. He still didn't understand how any cat could love water or what had motivated Merlin to learn to swim, much less hold onto a kite, while he sank his rear claws into a board so he could surf it across the harbor. But, ever since moving aboard Whispurring Winds, he'd realized anything related to water sports would be good skills to learn in his new environment. And, no matter how much it disgusted him, he'd made every effort to become as proficient on the water as he was on land.

However, unlike Merlin, he'd never learned to love anything about being wet.

Xander shook his head so hard his ears flattened. He

didn't have time to reminisce about the past; he had to find a way to pacify the Purrsident, even though he couldn't possibly do much purrsonally, no matter how much the Purrsident had stressed her wish. The solution was to find a way for Sir Simon to handle the situation. He turned his attention to the laptop and studied the tom's qualifications. Odd that the tom had undergone a frontal declawing, he couldn't think of another purrtector who didn't have all his claws. How in Catamondo could the tom protect himself in a brawl?

Perhaps he really needed help.

Xander leaned closer to the monitor to reread a few other lines in the file. Eighteen-inches at the shoulder and forty-two from nose to tail ... but only thirteen-pounds? Xander blinked in disbelief. How could the tom be an inch taller and a full half-foot longer and weigh eight pounds less? Didn't Jamaican humans know how to cook for their owners? If the Intel was right, the boy was nothing but fur covered bones. He wondered if a tom that light would need a kite to surf.

Xander closed his eyes and shook away the errant thought. He needed to figure out why the tom had involved the Purrsident.

Why Lady Montgomery had involved him was obvious: he was the best and he was in the general area – the Purrsident simply didn't understand how huge the general area was.

Xander scrolled down to view the kid's credentials. Unless the records were missing vast parts of Simon's file, the kid was an interpreter for kitten's stories, who might be able to spell the word kick, but probably didn't know how to execute one. Xander's eyes crossed. How in Catamondo had the tom gotten his appointment? Did the Jamaicans think the guy could right wrongs because he was literate?

The best way for him to cover his tail would be for Simon to resolve the situation.

The question was: if Simon was capable and if not, how could he manage the situation from the middle of nowhere?

Chapter 2

He was the only one awake in the dark, clinging night.

At least he hoped he was.

Perhaps that was what he was meant to think.

Before doubts could bind him, Xander leaped onto a pile of trampoline-like netting at C Pause's bow. After landing on feather-quiet paws, he made his way to the starboard side, then picked his way past stinking black bags of trash that covered most of the double-hulled vessel's solid decks. The smell had been bad before, but as he slid from shadow to shadow, it became overpowering. He held his breath, mostly due to the stench, but partially listening for sounds of movement. The only thing his sensitive hearing picked up was the soft beat of his own heart and the even fainter rhythms of five others.

Now that he could see from a new perspective, he again studied the boat's rigging, looking for motion-sensor cameras, or anything else a dog might install to spy with. Either Valentine was better at camouflaging a security system than he was or C Pause didn't possess any electronic technology. In fact, the motorboat's meager rigging was devoid of everything except seagull poop.

Xander sat in a stinking shadow, wondering if the lonely antenna was meant to lull him into carelessness and if the stench was meant to repel unwanted interest as well has encourage others to hurry by. He took his time studying the bulging black bags for any clue about why someone would turn their deck into a stinking garbage dump.

Ginny referred to C Pause as a packrat's paradise. He inhaled, but didn't detect any hint of rodent. Breathing lightly while listening to the night, he inched around the two rusty bicycles tied to the lifelines, then carefully avoiding all puddles and piles left by the mutt, moved toward the cockpit. The boat should be called a dog-doo-cruiser, instead of a motorboat, so the proper credit for the filth was apparent.

An odd groaning sound made his hair stand on end. Not a whimper and not a growl, it wasn't like anything he'd ever heard. He stopped in mid-step and waited.

The stars inched across the sky, but the noise didn't come, again. Xander convinced himself it was safe to go on. Now that he was past the bags of garbage and bikes, seven yellow five-gallon cans of diesel were the next hazard. That stuff always made him sneeze, so he held his breath while he maneuvered around them. Then he inched past a snarl of line, which looked moldy in daylight, but appeared silvery in the faint moonlight. With the threat of a sneeze past, Xander carefully inhaled as he ghosted past a last huge glistening black bag and inadvertently inhaled the foul aroma of rotting onion. Nose cringing, eyes watering, he hurried toward his objective, uncaring about stealth.

How could anyone live like this?

Why would they choose to?

Oddly enough, no one was keeping watch, not even

someone napping when they were supposed to be on watch. Fur quivering at the thought of going into the hull he stood still until he got past his fear of getting trapped inside the unknown. He leaned close to the open door. A ticking clock punctuated the feather-soft sound of breathing; three heartbeats varied rhythm; the scuttle of tiny feet as bugs moved through the refuse.

Hathor, please free Whispurring Winds from this infested boat before the vermin infested my home!

The groan came, again and for a moment it seemed the goddess was speaking directly to him. His fur leapt to attention and it took an act of will not to run.

The sound ended in an ungodlike whimper.

Discretion being the better part of valor, Xander retraced his steps until he reached the foredeck, then he dodged sideways to a spot on the upper deck, where the shadow of Whispurring Wind's mast screened him, yet allowed a good view of the cluttered deck without being cornered. He peeked into an open porthole. After several heartbeats, he moved to the next porthole, then the next, each offering less and less cover, until peering down, he spotted Valentine sprawled on his back, legs splayed with paws twitching. Xander closed his eyes to block out the revolting sight, but it was too late; the vision would undoubtedly give him nightmares.

Lids clinched, Xander entered the Zen state he needed to conduct a proper investigation. Then, he slowly opened his eyes and made certain the boxer was actually sleeping, instead of playing 'possum. Satisfied that conditions were as good as possible, he made a through inspection of the topside, paying particular attention to the bulging bags, which had been tied to the lifelines when he had first seen the boat. C Pause looked very different from his own Whispurring Winds, where nothing unnecessary came aboard and all nasty things left as soon as possible.

Why hadn't they dumped the rubbish?

Was it really waste or merely meant to appear like foul trash? If garbage wasn't in the bags, what was?

He studied the way the thick black plastic had been tied, wishing that he dared to take the time to undo the intricate knots and peek inside. The complex fastening convinced him that whatever was inside probably was not trash and was much more likely to be some sort of contraband, which they were braZen enough to hide in plain sight.

Whiskers twirling, he recalled a dingy he had seen in Cartagena's harbor – no one had wanted to tie their dingy near it at the dock because it had looked too old and rusted and been covered in seagull poop. Strangely, it had not smelled bad ... He had politely asked the vessel's cat-owner why he allowed his humans to be so slovenly. Reese had laughed loud and long. "Camouflage," Reese had managed to say, then he had laughed for a good minute before he managed to control his emotions and explain that outboard motors were a hot commodity and frequently stolen, so his humans had used lacquer paint to visually age their brand new, high power outboard, then topped it with a caulk, to simulate poop. In the year and a half since they had made the visual modifications, they had never had any problems with thieves.

Xander turned his attention back to the poop, sniffed and nearly gagged. Not caulk.

That still didn't mean it hadn't been left to distract attention from something else.

Cautiously, he made his way homeward. As he neared one of the three cleats, which held one of the lines fastening the two boats together, his claws itched to sink into the Dacron again and again, until it weakened enough to allow the boats to drift apart, as had the painter Cha-Cha damaged. But she'd spent weeks fraying that one and someone would certainly catch him before he had time to simulate adequate chaffing to explain C Pause's disappearance. Worse, he'd need to work on all three lines and calibrate it so they ripped simultaneously, which required more effort that he could afford to spend when he had a red claw crisis to deal with.

A red claw situation superseded the destruction of three potential cockroach highways – even when the disgusting bugs could end up in his own kibble.

Experience told him his humans would untie the lines at their first opportunity, he hoped it would be soon enough to avoid infestation and they would never see C Pause, again. After sparing the lines another glance, Xander hoped onto his own pristine deck, breathed in clean, salty air to clear the putrid stench from his lunge, and finally, he checked on Ginny and Mike both of whom were sleeping far too serenely for his peace of mind. After verifying the boring sameness of the screen, he left the deck's salty sheen and with nothing to keep him from addressing the current situation, he sat down at his laptop.

Whiskers twirling, he glared at the screen. How could one rub heads with a flat screen monitor to give a proper hello to a complete stranger? His tail twitched. Since e-mail lacked the ability to convey true thoughts and feelings, like a greeting, he could use this as an advantage.

Xander flexed his claws then carefully typed: Simon, then sat back, wondering if his greeting was too rude, even for e-mail. Despite the tom's lack of medals won in competition and the boy's glaring lack of training, the Purrsident, herself, had referred to him as Sir Simon. Surely, there must be more than one cat in Jamaica, so the boy must have been elected to his position. Xander's whiskers quivered as he recalled all the times his humans had moaned about voting against the 'lesser of the two evils instead of someone they truly wanted'. He hoped Simon's election didn't suggest feline culture was falling to the level of human society.

Regardless for the reason the tom occupied the position, he did hold it and that qualified him to be addressed as Sir.

Nose wrinkled to half its normal length, Xander added the proper greeting of respect:

> Sir Simon,
>
> Lady Montgomery asked me to assist you in any way possible so you may achieve a happy conclusion in the catnapping of Dame Esmeralda. Unfortunately, I am currently two to three sailing days away with a good wind. Unfortunately, at present there

is no wind, so I am only able to research
this situation from a distance.

Do you have any additional
information about the crime than you
sent to Lady Montgomery? I ask this
because I understand that while it
was necessary to report this crime,
you might not have felt certain details
were necessary for her to know.

Do you have reason to believe that Dame
Esmeralda was injured during the incident?

Have you been able to confirm if a ransom
has been demanded? If so, who would get
this – I ask because I understand her human
passed away recently and do not know
if she has obtained a new one.

If no ransom has been demanded, have you
been able to deduce the reason for the
 catnapping?

There is ALWAYS a reason for anything that
man or beast does.

Have you purrsonally spoken to
 eyewitnesses?

Please forward any and all information you
have to this address

I have begun analysis of the situation and will arrive as soon as felinely possible.

Regards,

Kamakaze Xander de Hunter, Sea Purrtector

He stretched and reread his missive. Not knowing if the kid would let the Purrsident know he'd responded and was moving as fast as his present situation allowed, Xander carbon copied the note to Lady Montgomery, lastly he inserted his seal of office. Then, with a flick of a claw, he sent it.

He spent the remainder of the night researching Jamaica's geography and crime history. By the time the first rays of sun peeked through the eastern porthole, he suspected that Jamaica was one of Dogdom's strongholds and that the catnapping was a power move, and not something for profit.

No wonder the situation had merited The Red Claw!

Chapter 3

Fifty-five hours later, Xander sat on his foredeck watching Jamaica's distant mountains materialize in a rugged blue line on the horizon. He shivered with foreboding. Why couldn't some sort of resolution have been achieved while he still had hundreds of miles of miserable water separating him from that hostile land and the situation that could cost him his reputation?

Ginny came on deck and began hoisting the yellow piece of fabric she called a 'Q flag'. The quarantine flag signaled immigration authorities that they intended to land. Once his boat had been properly processed and inspected, Ginny or Mike would take down the 'Q' and hoist the 8" x 10" replica of the Jamaican flag, which Ginny had painted. Having the country's flag flying showed that his boat had been properly processed and was legal. This eliminated many political problems, but it also created a record of where Whispurring Winds was as well as the dates he was in a specific country; and if his suspicions about Jamaica being a canine stronghold were fact, then official documentation gave them information he would have preferred they didn't have.

And he would bet his flea collar that he was about to enter a canine controlled port.

His stomach knotted with the certainty that he purrsonally

needed to do something about Dame Esmeralda. Or at least appear to do something, about the trail, which had gone cold somewhere on the other side of those distant blue mountains.

Whiskers drooping, Xander went below and studied the chart lying on the table for what seemed like the hundredth time. No matter how many times he examined the maps, Jamaica looked like a harsh rock stuck in the Caribbean Sea. Hoping that a closer inspection would reveal more roads or at least something good, he climbed onto the table, sat on top of the chart and began by scrutinizing the area surrounding Port Antonio's marina, where he would land. Though it lay less than a tail's length from Kingston, where the crime had taken place, the island appeared to have more rivers than roads. He shuddered at the possibility of still needing to use boats to get around once he got on land.

Xander focused on the thin gray line meandering along the shore before it zigzagged into the mountains. While it appeared to be the main road, it certainly didn't have the feel of an interstate. Puerto Rico's interstate hadn't been anything like home, and some of the side roads Mike had driven over had potholes so large that Mike literally drove the rental car into them, then out the far side. He shuddered at the memory. One hole had been large enough to bury most of a pickup truck, that had gotten stuck in the bottom as the tide came in.

He had quickly learned that road quality varied drastically when their rental car had gone airborne rocketing out of one of Puerto Rico's huge potholes. Since Jamaica was even smaller than Puerto Rico and the maps showed fewer roads, he feared the roads could be smaller and the holes larger.

He closed his eyes and controlled his breathing. What would be would be and worry would not change the situation.

The mansion from which Dame Esmeralda had been catnapped was on the south side of the island, while Port Antonio was on the north shore. Somehow, he needed to find a nice dry way to get to the scene of the crime, but it didn't look promising. He slapped the chart with his tail.

Mike put down his book. "Off the table. You know better than that!"

Xander hopped down, shocked at being caught, embarrassed at being so upset by the situation that he hadn't paid attention to the obvious fact that Mike was less than ten feet away.

Details were important, more than most ever realized.

Xander sprinted back into the cockpit, hopped onto the rail, squinted at the island's peaks and assured himself that the distance across such a rugged land would be as good a reason for him not to become any more directly involved than he had been from the middle of the sea. Surely he could continue to use the Internet to answer Sir Simon's constant questions about how to solve the crime.

By the time Ginny piloted Whispurring Winds through the narrow channel into a pretty round harbor, Xander had convinced himself everything would be fine. A seagull swooped through the air and screeched, as if congratulating him on his insight. He blinked in surprise. After spending the past three months in the Bahamas, he hadn't realized how much he'd missed watching gulls — birds in general, for that matter. Not that there weren't birds in the Bahamas, he'd heard a few singing in the short hardy shrubbery which cloaked the dry rocky little islands, but there certainly hadn't been any silly, self-important gulls.

As Ginny pulled into a slip at the marina's dock, three humans rushed from a large colonial-style building to catch the lines Mike threw. Within minutes Whispurring Winds was secured to the concrete and wood dock. While Mike stood on the forward deck chatting, Ginny placed their three fat white bumpers between the fiberglass hull and the rough dock. Assured that they were doing their jobs properly, Xander watched gulls swoop into the water, and come up with nothing but claws dripping water. At last, one gull caught a thrashing silver fish, but as it struggled to regain altitude and reach shore, it was bombarded by its relatives. As they fought for the frantic fish, it dropped back into the dark water with a silvery flash, twisted once, then disappeared. Ah, yes, he'd definitely missed watching those stupid birds. Xander inhaled the strangely scented air.

"You're The Great Kamikaze, aren't you?"

Startled that someone had managed to sneak up on him, he played it cool as he slowly turned to face a cute black and white feline with huge golden eyes, who was sitting on the dock. "I'm Xander."

"I knew it! I knew it! I knew it!" Whiskers twirling with excitement, she danced a little jig. "Just wait 'til I tell everyone that you're here! Of course, Simon knew you'd come, but everyone thought he was simply certifiable. It's like you're the most amazing tom, but I guess everyone tells you that, don't they?"

He smiled, uncertain about how to respond, then what she'd said sank in. "You know Simon?"

"Well, of course. Simply everyone knows him."

This was not the best news. "So it's easy to get to Kingston from here?"

"Oh, I wouldn't know." She gave him a huge smile. "The Omaha say, 'Ask questions from your heart and you will be answered from the heart'."

Was the girl daft or had he missed some sort of cultural nuance concerning a locally important family named Omaha? Xander tried, again, "Isn't Kingston where Simon lives?"

"If you say so." Another smile. "You aren't afraid of anything, are you?"

"Why do you say that?"

"Well, I've never met any cat that actually stood on deck when their boat came into port, but there you were, bigger than life – well, not really bigger, because you're really the size you are, but you know what I mean – there you were right up there on deck, talking to Julio and not being a bit afraid of him mistaking you for a fish and trying to bite you or anything. And you named the boat, didn't you?"

"I beg your pardon?" She looked up. So did he. "Are you referring to that seagull?"

"Well, of course I am! Oh, stupid bird that he is, he probably didn't give you his name, did he? Of course he wouldn't because birds never seem to understand the proper way to greet anyone or even know what to do or say when they do." Xander stared at her in amazement, noting that the bird was not the only one who had failed at displaying proper protocol. "I think you're the most amazing tom I ever met. Coming here and sitting right there in the open, chatting with Julio and Hathor only knows what goes through that bird's mind."

"Seagulls interest me." Her eyes widened, so he explained, "I find the way they always seem to act pompous amusing particularly because they never really manage to be." Gads, he was starting to be as much of a gabby tabby as whats-her-name was. "Excuse me, but I don't recall your name."

Her pale pink nose deepened to red and she lowered her gaze. "Sharkey." He leaned forward to hear her as she addressed the concrete wharf. "Actually, it's really Shark Bait, but my humans generally called me Sharkey and acted like they really like being owned by me." By now, she seemed to be muttering more to her paws than talking to him. He didn't know how to respond to this, so said nothing. After all, what could he say to a girl named Shark Bait? "I know it's a horrid name, but it's the only one I've ever had."

She seemed so miserable, he looked around for something else to talk about, but thoughts of consoling her were forgotten when he saw C Pause's red prow coming into the harbor. Hathor help him, the last thing he needed was to deal with Valentine, particularly when the mutt might overhear gabby Ms. Sharkey, who knew his title and reason for being in Jamaica. Xander leaped onto the dock, landing lightly next to her. "How about you show me your town?"

"Me?" Her voice squeaked. "You don't mind being seen with me?"

He looked her up and down. "Why should I?"

"But everyone around here knows my name!"

"So?" She blinked in confusion. He had to get her moving

before Valentine got close enough to see which way they'd gone. "I think Sharkey is a cute name. It sure beats Hairball." He took a step toward the main pier.

She snorted. "No one would ever have that name."

"Wanna bet?" Her gaze met his and when she saw his sincerity, her eyes widened. "Look, if you really don't like it, give yourself a new name."

"Like what?"

"Whatever makes you happy. Now, how's about that tour?" He started toward the huge white building with the two-story high pillars. "And while we're at it, tell me everything you know about the area and country." Without giving her a chance to disagree, he picked up his pace. She caught up with him as he stepped under bushy plant with loads of orange blooms. "Interesting plant."

"Watch out for thorns." Her warning was a second too late. He paused and pretended to study the blossoms, though he was actually checking out Valentine's position and determining a safe retreat. "Sometimes butterflies come to them," Sharkey went on, "but not often. I guess that's not surprising because there aren't all that many butterflies around here. I bet you have lots of butterflies."

"On a boat?" he asked, startled.

"No, back in North America. You did have plants and stuff there, didn't you?" He stared at her. Did she think he'd come from the moon or some other strange place? She shifted from paw to paw. "You did live in the United States, didn't you?" She hurried to add, "I'm nearly positive I read that."

He inclined his head. "Of course, we had bugs, birds, squirrels. toads and all sorts of stuff there. but I've been living on Whispurring Winds for a long time and none of the Bahamian Islands I've seen in the past weeks have had fresh water. So, yes, I'm originally from the U S, but it has been a while since I've seen nice plants." She looked like she didn't know how to take his comment. Worse, being reminded of his lovely woodland home brought nostalgic memories. Xander missed the way the gulls made so many unsuccessful attempts to catch the koi in his old pond, he missed the wrens who lived near the back porch and the way they sang to him; he missed the way the bees buzzed around the vegetable garden happily humming as they worked. And he missed being able to rub noses with Fluffy. He'd spent many lovely afternoons sharing his favorite sun-warmed napping place, with her while they listened to the peaceful symphony of nature, nibbled catnip leaves and planned the best way to train their respective humans.

Now, he had salt-slick decks, sometimes mosquitoes or itty-bitty-biting bugs, and occasionally flying fish, which appeared with the dawn.

It was no wonder he felt so stressed out by the red claw situation that hung over him like a dismal fate when he had no way to relax and see his way through problems or someone to bounce ideas against. He shook his head to help orient himself.

"Are you feeling okay?" Sharkey asked.

"Certainly," he said, but her expressive eyes told him that she could see the lie, so he admitted, "I still feel like I'm bouncing about on the waves." Her eyes widened with concern. "Mike gets this feeling, too. He calls it landsickness." Sharkey sat down with a graceless thump. "It's not contagious," he assured her.

For several moments, they sat side-by-side in the shade of the papery thin orange and pink flowers and watched a black butterfly with yellow spots flutter from one blossom to the other. "I've heard of seasickness," she said softly.

He nodded. "It's more common, but ultimately the same problem." She looked at him, her expression confused. "For seasickness, a cat can't adjust to the movement of the boat ... it takes me a day or so to get used to the ground not moving." He gave her a small smile.

"You really are a tom of the sea, aren't you?" Admiration suffused her tone.

Was he? Xander batted an ear. "I'm working on it." C Pause nosed into a slip on the other side of a powerboat. If he wanted to leave without Valentine seeing which way he'd gone, now was the ideal time, even if it felt like a gerbil was careening around in his stomach. "The best way to get used to being on solid ground is to walk." He stood up. So did she. With a flick of his ear, he indicated that she should lead the way.

Without being prompted, she took a serpentine route through the lush shrubbery, which surrounded the building. Pleased with the route she'd taken to mask their movements from everything but the most dedicated spy network, he waited to see what she'd do once they got past the thriving vegetation. Several feet before the road, she suddenly sat down and began to identify the various plants around them, then she walked to the base of a huge tree. "This is a breadfruit tree, unlike bananas and coconuts, they're worth climbing." It reminded him of a white oak he'd often sharpened his claws on.

Xander stood on his hind legs, ripping at the bark, feeling better every moment. When his shivs were razor-sharp, he retracted them. Sharkey was staring at him, her eyes as big as saucers. "That was so amazing."

"Don't you sharpen your claws?"

"Well, of course. I mean who doesn't? But you ... I've never seen anyone do the chore with such speed and style. I can certainly see how you earned your titles." She lowered her gaze and batted a piece of bark he'd shredded from the trunk. "I'm chatting on, aren't I? And you're so gallant about not telling me to shut up because you have landsickness. Sorry about that, it's just that I'm so excited about actually seeing you, let alone talking to you and you to me, like I'm somebody important or something."

"Everyone is important." She gave a slight shake of her head. "Seriously, it's all in the definition. For instance, if someone only likes one thing, they'll only think that is important, and if someone else likes something different, they will never understand the first feline. And who is to say which one is correct and which one is wrong?"

She raised her head revealing golden eyes round with wonder. "But how could you possibly think I'm important?"

"For one thing, you live here, so you know this area." He studied her. "Would you be willing to help me while I'm here?"

"Me?" Sharkey looked ready to faint. "You want me to help you?"

"I don't know anyone more qualified," he assured her. She shook her head so hard her ears flattened. "You knew this was a breadfruit tree." He kept his voice calm. "You told me banana and coconut trees were worthless things to climb."

"No branches," she murmured.

"Well, how am I supposed to gain insider knowledge of things like this without someone like you?" She looked at him, still unconvinced. "I research what I can think to ask, but it never occurred to me that some local trees might not have branches. There must be all sorts of information you know about this place that I'll need." She sat up a bit straighter. Xander smiled. It felt good to make the cute little gal feel better about herself, even if he doubted that he'd ever need to know about bark quality of local trees since it was obvious which ones had branches, which had leaves large enough to hide in and which had such thin leaves that even a wren couldn't hide in its boughs.

A chorus of barking erupted near the marina. He studied the area they'd just come from, to see what the dogs were up to. Across the harbor, four rail-thin brown dogs ran onto a barely visible sandbar. Noses high, they appeared to be shouting to Valentine, who stood looking at them from C Pause's bow. Ears straining, he tried to understand the dialect.

"Don't mind that riffraff," Sharkey's nose wrinkled. "They're just begging from the fat red one."

"You don't think much of them," he observed. With a twitch of her ear, she agreed. He studied the scraggly pack some more. Their location was ideal to observe the comings and goings of the harbor – things they probably report to dog central along with the more important information. And, like the worst novice, he'd been standing on the bow when Whispurring Winds sailed past their spy-post. By now, every dog on the planet probably knew exactly where he was. And, assuming they were involved in the catnapping, they almost certainly knew why he'd come to Jamaica. The more they spoke in code with Valentine, the more certain Xander became that the annoying red boxer was spying on him and the more he began to recognize that sneaking aboard Whispurring Winds on the night he'd received the red claw alert might have been more cunning than coincidence.

And if Valentine's sneaky visit had been planned, then it stood to reason that the dogs were definitely behind Dame Esmeralda's abduction and the entire situation could be a trap for him to reveal himself, or Catamondo's Purrtector Network… at very least a way to ensnare poor Simon in a mess he had no hope of winning, which would bring down one Purrtector. Since Simon did not appear to be the most able Purrtector in Catamondo, and since Dame Esmeralda was Lady Montgomery's littermate, Xander understood why the canines had chosen to test the Purrtectors in Jamaica.

Valentine issued a command to the thin brown mutts; the four mongrels turned with military precision and disappeared into the mangroves – presumably to issue some sort of report. With that sort of cowering obedience, Valentine must be higher in Dogdom than he'd thought possible for anything that smelled so vile.

He needed to find better agents to infiltrate the dogs' network. Now that he'd unmasked Valentine, he'd have to keep a steady eye on him, when it was possible – it simply wasn't feasible when he needed to get away from the dogs' not-so-secret agent without leaving any trial.

But how could he get away from the boxer and help Simon foil the dogs' evil plan?

He looked around, his gaze settling on the freshly scared trunk. Hathor, what had he been thinking when he left such an obvious sign? He might as well have shot off a flare!

The white under-bark blazed like a beacon. This was the second time today he'd done something so stupid that even the youngest kitten would know better. He looked heavenward, barely noticing the thick, strong branches and the way many of them interlaced with vines and other trees. Then, inspiration struck. "Ever climbed this one?"

She blinked in such an odd way as she peered skyward that he wondered if she'd ever climbed a tree. "Must be a grand view from up there."

"Bet you're right." Without waiting a moment more, he sank all claws into the trunk and hurried upward, fully expecting her to run home before anyone missed her. Halfway to the top, he dashed out onto a limb, which intersected with a huge branch from the next tree. He moved from tree to tree in this way a doZen more times, each new tree taking him farther away from the marina, until he couldn't even see the harbor. Knowing there wasn't a dog born that could track him through the boughs, he slowed his pace to enjoy the unexpected adventure. After his arboreal path took him over the ridge, there were more houses and fewer trees, so he had to slow down enough to plan his route. By the time the sun was high, he'd worked his way to the other side of town.

Before he got any father, he needed a plan.

Xander sprawled on a comfortable branch which offered a view of the most traveled road, yet camouflaged him behind wide, green, fiddle-shaped leaves. Slowly, he eased into a Zen-like state and let his mind run free.

"They should call you Tarzan!" a familiar voice said. A red-orange flower larger than her head lay wilted across her back, trapped by a cobweb, which had snagged her right ear.

"What happened to you?"

"Wadya mean?" Sharkey asked.

He sat up and carefully removed the flower. "Oh. That musta happened when I took that wrong turn in the Flame of the Forest."

Xander's fur tingled. "You went through fire?"

"Whatever gave you that idea?" He arched a brow. "Oh. No. Flame of the Forest is the name of the tree that those flower grows on." She gently tapped the limp petal. "I think it's 'cause the color makes it look like the trees are on fire."

"Fascinating."

"So, whatcha doing here?"

"Studying patterns." He curled his tail around his toes as he assumed his most dignified professorial posture. "How often do you look up?"

"You mean when I hear a bird?"

"Anytime."

Sharkey thought hard. "Not too often," she admitted, shamefaced. "That's the lesson, isn't it? Being up in a tree is a good place to watch from because no one looks up here to see who is watching them, so they go on about their business like regular."

"Precisely. You're smart to understand." Her eyes gleamed like polished brass. "It's best to get comfortable and be as quiet as possible." Without needing to be more blunt, Sharkey settled herself on the branch. The kid had potential, he thought as he returned to his Zen-state.

Chapter 4

Two hours before sunset, Xander made his way back through the boughs to the breadfruit tree. Valentine was executing a search pattern around the trunk. Xander's interest perked. There was definitely more to the mutt than advertised. Xander quietly maneuvered down to a wide limb, which offered an unrestricted view of the flabby red boxer, then sprawled on it and watched the dog as he continued circling the tree. After twenty-two laps, that Xander was there to observe, Valentine took two paces away from the trunk, and nose to the grass, started another larger circle. Ten laps later, Valentine again, took two paces away, and began sniffing the next larger circle.

Xander lost interest in the fruitless search, so took the opportunity to study the harbor from his concealed vantage point, paying particular attention to C Pause and the area where the thin, troop of dogs had gone.

Long past the point where any other cat would have confronted the snoop, Xander waited; he wanted to see how far Valentine would go. Suddenly Valentine gave a dreadful yelp, yanked his nose out of the grass and began running in tight, frantic circles yelling something about a bee. A moment later, he dashed into some nearby shrubbery and his howls of pain seemed to get farther away, but Xander knew how easy it was to modulate sound and trick opponents, so he made a big production of standing up, arching his back and yawning, as if he had just awakened from his afternoon siesta.

Casually, he sheathed half his claws and descended the tree trunk with as many clumsy slips and grabs as possible. Then, he awkwardly slipped the last two feet and landed in an undignified plop. A sneak peak confirmed that Valentine's attention was on him, so he stayed in the undignified position for fifty heartbeats, before staggered to his paws and began a lurching walk toward Whispurring Winds. After several steps, he tripped over his own paws and sat down hard.

He made an inelegant effort at cleaning his fur and pretended to notice Valentine, who was lurking behind a pink hibiscus bush. Xander feigned surprise because It never hurt to make the enemy think he was clumsy. "What are you doing here?" Xander widened his eyes and looked up at the branches, as if embarrassed. "Been there long?"

"No." Valentine took a step forward. "Heard some yelling, came to see what was going on."

"Yelling, huh? That must be what woke me up." Xander yawned. "Sounded like someone had died." He licked his paw and smoothed the fur on his face.

Valentine stood up, then moved a step forward, but stopped when he was half under the bush, half in front, which looked totally stupid.

He realized he wasn't the only one putting on an act to appear dumber than he actually was. Xander avoided looking at the swelling sting on the icky black nose and continued grooming himself. "Do you think we should look for whoever was yelling? I heard they have some demon thing call a chupacabra, that kills things." He tried to look frightened as he glanced around the area. "Do you think this place is safe?"

The dog puffed up with importance. "It's just you and me, now."

"So no chupacabra?"

Valentine shook his head so hard that great drops of spittle sprayed the area. "Just checking to make sure you're okey-dokey."

Xander stood up, stretched and yawned before he replied. "I feel better than I have in ages. Musta been the great nap I had." He gave another huge yawn, then sat down as if the only thing he wanted to do was chat with a red mutt. "You should try it sometime. There's simply nothing as relaxing as swaying on a sun drenched branch with birds singing."

"Don't you get enough of that living on a sailboat?"

"It's not the same at all." Valentine looked at him as if he was daft. "No leaves, no bark, and the birds definitely aren't the same. Not that there were many birds in the Bahamas." Valentine wasn't the only one gifted at playing stupid. He got to his paws and began walking toward the boat, making certain to walk like a drunken sailor. Valentine fell into step beside him. "Do you think chupacabras kill cats?"

"Never heard of one."

"Well, they sound dangerous, but I've never heard of one climbing trees." Xander stumbled, then pretended to clumsily catch his balance on shaky legs. "Have you listened to those birds with the yellow tummies? Very nice song. Not as lovely as the osprey in the Chesapeake, but lovely just the same."

"Yeah, but the bird you were up there with didn't have wings."

"I beg your pardon?"

Though Xander knew his posture didn't give him away, he was now on full alert, wondering how the mutt knew about Sharkey, who had traveled to her home by a different route. And even more tantalizing question was why the mutt was giving away his edge.

Valentine tapped his nose. "You can hide, but I know."

"I'm sure you know lots of things, but what is it that you supposedly know that you think I know?" The devious dog tried to look dumber than he already did. No dog was that dumb. Xander was convinced the dog was putting on an act.

"You know that wingless bird. You were up there with a girl."

Xander laughed. "Sure I was." Valentine looked confused. Xander gestured toward the island, where he knew the pack of watchers lurked. "You'd have a lot better chance of meeting a girl of your persuasion than me. I saw them all running out to greet you like you were some sort of celebrity or something." He glanced back to gauge his reaction. The dog looked redder than normal.

"You saw them?"

Xander grinned. "Hard to miss. At first I thought they were running on water, then I realized there was a shallow sandbar." He gave him a big wink. "They sure did look happy to see you." Valentine shook his head so hard that slobber splattered.

"You're just saying that to distract me from the chick you were up that tree with."

Reggae music drifted over the harbor mingling scents of squalid dog, peppery chicken, moist soil and ganja. Except for the chicken, the country's stench mirrored everything he'd observed on C Pause. Perhaps that was one reason his would-be-pal/spy seemed so at ease. "Valentine," Xander said gravely as he stumbled onto the dock, "I assure you that I was not, nor have I ever been up a tree with a chicken." His tail twitched. "Next thing you'll be telling me is that I spent the day in a tree with a shark."

"That's stupid."

Xander raised a brow. "Is it?" His tail twitched harder. "I think it'd be a fascinating way to spend a day." He'd never realized how amusing it was to watch dogs squirm. "Okay, I'll be serious, since I know you know that sharks don't climb trees, I confess that I was up there with Shark Bait."

"You're weird and I'm going back to my boat."

"Was it something I said?" he asked, but Valentine left without responding. Xander tripped his way back home, then gave himself a high five, as he leaped aboard Whispurring Winds. After making certain no other dogs were in a position to see into the cabin and no sort of surveillance equipment had come aboard during his absence, he checked his e-mail.

Fluffy had sent a photo of herself modeling her new pink, diamond-studded collar, which contained an amazing array of technology, which allow her to access data no matter where she was. Xander had a blue version, which matched his eyes. Though diamonds were part of the technology, he could not imagine wearing all that sparkly stuff, fortunately the research and development division had made his collar with gems that looked like sapphires.

There were only twelve collars with the advanced technology. Now, he, Merlin and Fluffy each had one because they were chief purrtectors of a large geographical area. However, Catamondo's R and D division had made certain that cheap knock-offs flooded the market, so the dogs would not be able to pick out the purrtectors simply by looking at their collars.

Xander quickly wrote Fluffy a note of congratulating her for her new collar.

Merlin wrote that he'd given into his sister's begging and had agreed to give Cha-Cha parasailing lessons.

The purrsident was on the cover of the on-line version of Cat Lovers magazine.

Cha-Cha wrote that Merlin was the most stubborn chauvinistic cat she'd ever met, but the good news was that she'd finally gotten through his thick skull. The bad news was that he had put her into a training class for six-week-old kittens.

Simon confessed that he wasn't one bit closer to solving the catnapping than he had been when he had advised "LM" about the situation. It was beginning to look like the catnapping would never get solved unless he purrsonally got involved.

Since seeing C Pause enter the harbor, Xander had become certain Dame Esmeralda's catnapping was part of one of Dogdom's sinister plots. He needed to figure out what Dogdom was up to so he could effectively counter their scheme. Unfortunately, by now the clues had become muddled either by time or Simon's bungling, so no matter what he did, it would probably be impossible to fully analyze the situation, as it had unfolded from the beginning.

Therefore, he needed to step out of the catbox and find a different way to solve the situation.

To take his mind off his problems, he reopened the photo Fluffy had attached to her message. "Who's the one with the gaudy pink and glitz collar?" Xander whirled shocked that Sharkey had managed to sneak up on him, for the third time in eight hours. No other cat had ever managed to accomplish such a feat.

"A friend."

Sharkey sniffed with disdain. 'How come she looks so pleased about wearing an emblem of slavery?" His own blue collar suddenly felt snug, so he stretched his neck. Sharkey's attention never wavered from the screen. "Pink with diamonds is sooooo tacky." Xander thought it looked wonderful peaking out from the long tresses of her gorgeous gray fur. Unsure of Sharkey's real motives for meeting him, when he docked and uncertain how well she could keep a confidence, Xander did not dare to tell her that only a doZen cats had collars equal to the technology packed into Fluffy's and that they were collars of honor, not slavery.

His own dignified sapphire-studded collar was built using the most powerful technology available, and due to the remote areas he often found himself in, even included a satellite link. He studied the little black and white gal, recalling how stealthy she was and the way dogs seemed to ignore her. Could she be a double agent? His ears flattened before he could stop them. Was she baiting him to reveal the secrets of Catamondo's most secret technology? He shrugged, as if Fluffy's collar was of no consequence. "It makes her happy." Then, he looked away from the computer and casually sniffed the air. "Say, do you know where they're cooking that chicken?" She inclined her head in the affirmative. "Think they'd miss a couple pieces?"

Her eyes widened. "What are you suggesting?"

"You. Me. Dinner."

She sat down with a thump. "You want to be seen in public with me?"

"Is there a problem with that? I mean we've just spent a lovely day together." She apparently didn't know what to think. "Look, I'm tired of dry kibble and that chicken smells too good to pass up." She stared at him. "Do you have a problem against getting some?" He allowed his question to trail off, then remained silent hoping she'd find her voice.

Sharkey sniffed the air. "It's jerk."

"Well, it smells like chicken to me." He sniffed, again. "Haven't heard of jerk, but it sure smells like bird and bird of any sort is my purrsonal favorite – turkey, chicken, even duck – whatever. I'm certain jerk will taste as good as it smells."

She giggled. "Jerk is a peppery seasoning that can burn your tongue. They put it on everything, even that chicken you're smelling."

"Ah, so it IS chicken with spices." He smiled. "If it's too hot. anv added flavor on the outside can be taken off." He casually flicked a claw and shut down his email program. With another flick, he concealed his direct link to Catamondo's files. Then, he stood up and stretched. "How about it, are you going to have dinner with me or shall I simply follow my nose?" Sharkey headed for the door. "So, what's your favorite food?" he asked as they leaped in tandem to the dock.

"Fish."

He thought about the flying fish that he often found on deck. "Interesting flavor, but way too much effort for what you get."

"What do you mean?" She looked serious.

"Bones. Scales."

"I've never noticed any."

"Have you ever had an over-nighter?"

"Are they some sorta North American type?" As they strolled down the dock, he described the big-eyed fish that frequently lay dead on the deck in the morning. Her nose twitched with the slightest disdain. "I've never seen anything like that at the dock. Things with eyes on twigs, things with snapping claws, fish with huge razor teeth, yes, but what you're talking about sounds more like bait." He ducked under a thick-leaved vine covered with bunches of white trumpet-shaped flowers. "You really shouldn't go near that stephanotis when you're tracking dinner."

He looked back at her. "Why not?"

"Its strong smell overpowers everything else."

"No matter," he said, as if he didn't understand her point. "It's lovely in here and you know where we're going."

Once he was hidden in the shadows, he nonchalantly looked around to see how many dogs were monitoring him. Though he didn't see Valentine, two skinny canines on the island were watching Sharkey, who hadn't had the sense to follow him into the cover, which would make visual and scent tracking difficult. He shook his head at the way she could appear so competent one minute and dense the next. If she wasn't going to make any effort to confuse the spies, there was no reason for him to make the effort. With a flick of his tail that knocked a powerful dose of nectar onto his fur, Xander moved back into the sunlight. "Interesting plant."

She murmured in agreement while he looked around like a tourist. Hopefully the dogs would think he's merely another sightseer. And with any luck, if Sharkey really was some sort of secret agent, she'd believe e-mails about glitzy collars were merely about slavery. If he was right about Sharkey being a possible turncoat from Catamondo, the false impression would be good; if he was wrong, the impression would not matter. He tilted his head to the ancient wrought iron gate. The gate's padlock appeared to be permanently rusted shut and while the bars were wide enough for him and Sharkey to slip through, only the scrawniest dog could ever hope to follow their actual path. "Let's go this way." Without comment, she followed him. He adopted a stumbling, leisurely pace that ambled under several thorny bushes and zigzagged around various strong-smelling plants, as if the only thing on his mind was getting a close look at every new species of vegetation, instead of confusing even the best tracker; then as he rounded a large rock, near the tree-covered slope, he came nose to beak with a rooster.

The startled bird let out a thunderous squawk and flapped his glistening black wings as he lunged at him. Xander leaped to the side allowing the bird to charge past him – directly at Sharkey. Instead of jumping to the side, she leaped upward as if propelled by a rocket. The bird shrieked as it shot underneath her and then skidded to a stop. "Quick, up that tree," Xander said.

Before the rooster could collect itself, he was halfway to the first branch, Sharkey close on his tail.

"You know they can fly," she said as she leaped onto the lowest limb and ducked out of the bird's view.

"True, but they don't like to beat their wings against hard surfaces." He patted the wide branch they'd taken refuge on.

"Ah." She watched the rooster spin around, looking for them. When it's glistening black tail was toward them, she sprinted to a section where the branches were denser. "It's ironic, don't you think?" The bird's beady black eyes peered upward.

"What is?" he asked as he waited for the bird to lose interest.

"Getting trapped up a tree by a chicken when we'd intended to eat one for dinner."

"You think we're trapped?" She gave him a blank look. He gestured to the way the branches interconnected with the next tree and the next and onward, until those of a wide-leaved tree laid on a convenient roof. "After this morning, I thought you'd realize that when we're in a tree, we have options only available to a few special species." Beneath them, the rooster squawked and scratched angrily at the dirt providing an excellent distraction for any spying canine. "Shall we?" Without waiting for a reply, he set off, taking a route that kept the trunk between him and the dog-inhabited mangroves. It didn't take long to get to the corrugated steel roof. Once there, he moved swiftly across the exposed expanse of sun-warmed metal to the edge, which overlooked the town's main street. Xander lay on his stomach and peered down at the narrow, pot-holed road, which barely had space for two vehicles to pass. Thin cracked sidewalks and reeking slime-filled gutter were on either side of the pitiful road.

"Can't you figure out how to get down?"

"Of course." He flicked an ear toward the thick wooden electrical post that someone had set in the middle of the sidewalk. "I'm wondering why you're the only cat I've seen, here." And he was wondering if Port Antonio is some sort of special canine commune. From this vantage point, he counted fourteen dogs separating him from the tantalizing aroma of jerk chicken. The good thing about the dogs was that each one acted like a lazy reject. The bad thing was that at least two were obviously mothers and everyone knew not to come between a mother and her pups, but the worst thing was that he couldn't see any pups. "There sure are a lot of dogs here," he said.

"They seem to be everywhere, don't they?"

He nodded. It explained why a lone cat would be forced by circumstances to join in an unholy alliance with the enemy. "The dogs have an academy around here or something?" he asked casually. The last thing he needed was for Whispurring Winds to be docked next to a training center, especially when he might need to go away from his ship for a few days.

"Clive usually has a lot of puppies, but I've never noticed

many anywhere else."

Xander tried to look like he was merely chatting about a casual topic. "Who or what is Clive?"

"The Rastaman, who lives there." She pointed to the mangrove-covered area where Valentine had first spoken to the thin dogs. His attention narrowed on the grove, but he was too far away to see anything the dogs didn't want seen. That area was something he'd have to investigate after he sorted out Simon's situation. "Clive goes around looking for lost or abandoned puppies, then he takes them back on that." Sharkey indicated an odd flat thing fashioned with long circular yellowish pipes of varying diameter, each half in the water, a green plastic stacking bin was attached to the wider end. A similar yellow rod lay across its narrowest end.

He'd read about the narrow bamboo rafts that Jamacians used to navigate rivers, but this was the first he'd seen. "Weird raft," he muttered.

"It's typical."

"You're kidding."

She shook her head. "They're traditional. Humans even have pictures of them in those brochures asking exorbitant amounts to give tourists river rides."

"Humans pay for the strangest things," he said.

"You're one to talk." He raised a brow. "Don't give me that innocent look," Sharkey sputtered, "most cats don't choose to live on boats."

He didn't respond to her comment, or admit that the move had promoted him from Eastern U.S. Purrtector to become the first Sea Purrtector, which was Catamondo's largest purrtectorate. Sharkey walked toward the telephone pole, leaped across the narrow expanse and started down. The dogs lounging near the street didn't appear to react. Either they were the most highly trained dogs he'd ever observed, or they actually were totally lazy. He doubted the latter, which renewed his suspicions about Sharkey's motives for befriending him.

Had her delight at meeting him and her extravagant compliments masked the fact she was an agent for the enemy? Or was she simply a lone cat caught in the middle of a dog-infested town, who was eager for feline company?

It could be either, but until he knew for certain, he needed to exercise caution.

As he followed her down the slippery pole to the grimy street, the stench thickened. Once he got to the broken concrete, Xander gave as much attention to where he stepped as he did to observing the dogs, who gave every appearance of ignoring him.

"Hathor, but their training is good," he muttered.

"Beware of the man who does not talk, and the dog that does not bark." Before he could ask Sharkey what she meant by the odd statement, she darted to her right, entering a narrow, twisting alley, and then she ducked through a crack in a crumbling wall to her left. She suddenly paused behind the protection of a rusty barrel. Continuing the clumsy act, in case any dogs were watching, he bumped into her.

"Sorry," he whispered. The air around them smelled so strongly of chicken that he wondered if simply breathing could make a body gain weight ... if so, it could explain why some of the dogs appeared fat. But it didn't explain why so many were thin as rails. Intense training, might explain that, though.

"White or dark?" Sharkey asked. He studied her black and white fur. "Breast or thigh?" He blinked in confusion. "Chicken- meat – which type do you like best?"

Xander assumed a dignified look. "I said I was taking you to dinner." It was fun to disorient her, and strange to realize how little time she'd probably spent with other cats. Or, perhaps it wasn't such a surprise since she was the only feline he'd seen since landing on Jamaica. He peered around the container. A tall, thin dark-skinned man with a crocheted red, yellow and green hat topping greasy, disheveled braids used two thin bamboo sticks as he turned six fat birds over the flames inside a 55-gallon-barrel that had been repurposed into grill. By the time grease from fat splattered the man's silky purple shirt and course yellow pants, Xander knew which bird he wanted for dinner. The man with the matted hair and gaudy clothes kept looking out the wide-open wall that separated his homemade grill from the sidewalk. When a well-dressed couple walked by the cook shouted, "Best chicken in Jamaica, mon! Get you's now." When the couple hastened by, he stepped onto the sidewalk and shouted after them, "You not wanna make dah pretty lady cook tonight, do ya? Sure dare muss be bedder tings to do." The couple walked faster. The man turned his attention back to the grill and turned each bird. Grease hit the coals with a sizzling splat that sent flames around the chickens. Xander glanced around the rest of the smoky room. The cook went through the same routine with the next couple.

Having figured out the pattern, Xander whispered into Sharkey's ear. "Wait for me in the alley." She gave him a skeptical look, but obediently moved through the broken wall. As the shaggy chef launched into his spiel for the third time, Xander moved with the lightening speed he was known for. As he ricocheted off the far wall, he snatched the closest bird off the grill. No sooner did his paws meet the dirt floor, but he veered behind the barrel and ducked back through the broken wall, where Sharkey waited for him.

"That was amazing!" Her eyes shown. "He didn't even see you!" Xander set the bird down between them. "Listen, he's still hollering at those people."

"That was the idea." Even if she might be a spy, it felt good to let her know what he could do if he wanted to. "Eat up."

"I can't believe you got a whole bird." Her pretty pink nose flushed crimson. "I was going to see what I could find in the rubbish." She sank her teeth into a leg, before she said more.

After they were both stuffed, there was still meat clinging to the carcass, so Xander picked it up and carried it to where the closest dog lay curled near the alley. He laid it down, but the tan dog continued sleeping, so he shoved it close. The nose trembled. One jaundiced eye opened. Stealthily, Xander melted back into the shadows, then, he moved out onto the sidewalk, tipped over the trashcan next to the barrel-turned-grill, and dashed back into the alley with the cook in livid pursuit. He ran past the dog, who was now gnawing the bird, and ducked under a cabinet before the man rounded the corner.

The man skidded to a halt next to the dog and started screaming with fury.

The dog growled a warning.

The man kicked.

The dog lunged.

The man kicked, again.

The dog howled in pain.

Xander twirled his whiskers, pleased with the day's work.

"What I've heard about your fighting abilities is true, isn't it?" Sharkey tilted her head to the side.

"Depends on what you heard."

"Do you give everyone evasive answers?" He laughed and shrugged. "How come you seem to do dumb stuff sometimes, yet other times you're the smartest, quickest and most agile tom I've ever known?"

"What do you mean?"

"You do dumb stuff like marking that breadfruit tree before you climb it and a few other times I've thought you were going to trip over your own paws, then you turn around and do amazing stuff like grab a whole chicken and you're so fast and silent that we have time to dine before you frame that dumb dog."

"Landsickness, I guess," he said with a dismissive shrug. "It comes and goes."

Chapter 5

Reggae riffs collided against a rock 'n' roll beat, then slammed into jazz rhythms in an ear-cringing torrent of noise across the waveless harbor. But the din didn't drown out dogs barking in the mangroves. He looked at Sharkey, who was napping on the second best cushion in the salon. How she and his humans managed to block out the dog's racket was a mystery. When the dogs in the mangroves became quite, others on the far side of town began to howl. Xander's ears flattened against his head as he tried to block out the musical din and focus on what they were saying to see if it held a hidden message, but no sooner had he started to focus, than the dogs became quiet.

After several minutes, the barking resumed even farther away. A moment later, the closer ones started barking again, but it sounded like barking for the sake of making noise, not to cover a coded message.

Deep in thought about what the dog telegraph might mean to him, Xander opened his email. Simon had written an ingratiating thank you note to the Purrsident. The tom certainly had a gift for twisting words, since he managed to give the impression that he, Xander, would be solely responsible for any unwanted outcome. The urge to hiss at the e-mail expanded within his chest. He tore his attention from the infuriating letter and looked at Sharkey. Unwilling to blow his cover, he inhaled a deep breath through his nose, held it for the count of ten, then blew the combined anger and air out through his mouth.

He repeated the calming ritual twice before his sense of serenity overpowered the emotions Simon's message generated. Xander's tail thumped the cushion. If the tom's only intention was to dump the blame, he probably would not have sent him a copy of the email. With that thought in mind, Xander sat down and read every word of the note, which announced that the clues were leading him Northward. Xander switched to his map of Jamaica to look up the coordinates, which Simon listed as being the catnappers last known destination, then selected a convenient location to meet Simon, then e-mailed him the coordinates and told him to get there as fast as possible. Xander doubted that dogs were dumb enough to stay at any specific location for several days, unless they were the bait in a trap.

Xander keyed 17 30'N 76 47'W into his collar, did one last visual check of the map, then he smacked the esc key, killing Simon's message.

Sharkey opened an eye. "Something wrong?"

"What could be wrong? It's nearly 3 in the morning and I can't get any sleep because one band is belting out jazz while the other two are now blaring that reggae stuff and at least four packs of dogs are howling. What on earth could be wrong?"

She yawned. "So you're saying this isn't typical."

The way she made it a statement instead of a question gave him pause. "But it is for here?"

"Absolutely."

What a Hathor-awful place! "In that case, when does the music stop?"

She thought a moment. "Generally when all the roosters start crowing."

Dear Hathor, he'd forgotten about the dozens of those off-key birds that either congratulated themselves for staying alive to meet the sun or sleeping through the clashing music from three bands.

"Have dogs and poultry taken over every part of Jamaica?"

"Huh?"

"Never mind." He doubted the dogs were capable enough, let alone smart enough to accomplish that anywhere. Whatever was going on in other areas of the island had to be better than Port Antonio, which was obviously a town devoted to puppy training. "I guess I'd better get going."

"Where?"

He gave a slight shrug, listened to Mike snore for several moments, then said, "It doesn't matter as long as it's quiet enough to sleep."

Reluctantly, Sharkey stretched. "Ready whenever you are."

"Look, I really like your company, but you don't have to come with me." He tried to sound casual despite his relief at the idea of having her companionship. If she truly was a spy, she wouldn't be able to snoop while he was away and if she wasn't it could be handy to have someone as quiet as her around.

"Mon, yajusdonnaspeakdelingo."

He stared at her. "What'd you say?"

"You don't speak the local dialect – that's what I said, but I said it in Pawdama - and your question verified why I must come."

Xander's gaze narrowed, "How come you speak paw-whatever?"

Her whiskers twitched. "You really mean 'why haven't I spoken to you in Pawdama' and that's simple – its island lingo, you just arrived. Obviously you haven't had time to learn."

He studied her, realizing for the umpteenth time that there was more to this little black and white gal than he'd first suspected. It was something he'd look into when Valentine spying. Unfortunately, the mutt had just boarded and was eavesdropping outside the aft hatch. Did the fool mutt really think he couldn't hear his slobber splat against the deck? That he couldn't smell his rancid aroma? Xander snorted.

"What's wrong?" Sharkey asked.

"Nothing." Xander scratched his collar, which seemed heavier than usual. Her attention centered on the azure leather, her revulsion apparent. If her allegiance to Catamondo was certain and if Valentine hadn't been lurking nearby, he would have shown her how many things he could accomplish with the technology hidden in it. He tilted his head and looked at her. Assuming she was a spy, a demonstration might show her just how superior cats were so he could turn her into a double agent, but he wasn't fool enough to allow a dog to witness such power, no matter how tempting it was to impress a gal with the way Catamondo's best scientist had learned to alter collars, catnip mice and other common items to be much more than what the humans managed to make.

His ears flattened with irritation at the reminder of how many things he had to do to keep his people calmly ignorant of the truth – cats had been so successful in training their servants that most humans were silly enough to believe they owned cats when everyone knew it was vice-versa. He made certain the computer was exactly the way it had been when he'd sat down to work, hours before. In a perfect world, he wouldn't need to let them believe they'd chosen him. Of course, in a perfect world, his servants would never have done anything as radical as drug him on catnip, pop him into his carry-crate and move him aboard a boat. And less than two weeks before the global election – the election in which he'd been the favorite to win North American Purrtector. Not that their deed had ended badly – after explaining why he needed to exclude his name from the ballot, the Purrsident had convened a special session of the Global Council they had unanimously voted to create the position of Sea Purrtector and appointed him as the first – no election involved. He wondered if the Council had taken into account that 75% of the planet was flooded, which gave him a wider range of influence than any other feline, or if they figured that since there were so few cats per square mile of water, he had limited authority.

If so, they'd overlooked the fact that he'd spent the past few years developing internet technology and writing instructions so every cat with access to a computer could communicate with anyone else at any time. Moving aboard Whispurring Winds had actually added to his vast array of electronics, in large part due to his ability to integrate several technologies by using the HAMM radio. His nose wrinkled, as he thought how poorly named the black plastic gizmo was and how strange humans were to name something that useful, but inedible after a pig

Of course, humans always named things wrong: the black box reporters always spoke of on aircraft was actually bright orange; if they called someone Slim, he generally waddled; and they continually referred to 'common sense' when it was obviously the least common thing he'd ever seen in the human race.

"Something is really bad-wrong, isn't it?" Sharkey's golden eyes appeared larger than usual.

"Just thinking." He gave the cabin a final glance. "Guess if I want to find some peace and see this country, we'd better get going before it gets too hot." He strolled toward the cockpit, as if he didn't have anything more pressing in mind than sight-seeing. When she caught up with him on the steps to the cockpit, he asked, "What do you know about Kingston?"

Whatever she intended to say was forgotten when Valentine stepped in front of them. "You can't leave the boat."

"Are you putting me under arrest or something?"

"Not me," Valentine said ominously, "it's the law."

"Where's your badge?" Xander edged past him, making certain his fur didn't touch the mutt.

"Buddy, I'm telling you this for your own good. No animals are allowed off boats – we're in quarantine."

"That means you're supposed to be on your boat, not

mine."

"And I would be, if you didn't keep jumping ship!" Great globs of slobber blossomed along his jowls. "What am I gonna do without you?"

Sharkey, who was in the process of circumventing a glob of fallen spittle, stumbled into the putrid mess. Leaping back, she muttered, "Those that lie down with dogs, get up with fleas."

Valentine shot her a surprised look. Damned if the mutt wasn't a good actor, he almost believed the bit about his desire to protect his friend.

Sharkey straightened, "Is this dog a friend of yours?" Her tone sounded genuinely scathing.

If he denied it, Valentine would watch him twice as hard and if he didn't and Sharkey wasn't a spy, she would have something to gossip about – or worse. "Sharkey, this is Valentine. He lives aboard that boat." Giving his ear a disdainful slant, which dogs never understood, he pointed toward C Pause.

"So you were being honest!" Valentine sniffed Sharkey, then gave a deep woof of laughter. "You dog, you!"

Xander's shivs inched out, ready to rip the rude dog's nose to shreds. Sharkey's eyes narrowed as she divided her attention between them. "What are you talking about?" Xander demanded.

A roaring woof of laughter splattered globs of spit in a vile wave. Xander hastily stepped out of the way. Sharkey moved back into the salon and chose a spot where she could watch both of them, but not get involved or contaminated. "You said you were up that tree with a shark, and you weren't lying." Valentine looked like he'd just given the punch line to the best joke in the world, but he was the only one laughing.

"Those Blackfoot sure did have it right," Sharkey grumbled.

"What black foot?" he asked.

"You couldn't possibly understand." She defiantly raised her chin.

Acting as if he was totally disgusted, Xander went back down the ladder. Sharkey kept her attention on the wall, when he sat next to her. "Sorry," he said, "I should have warned you about that creep." She didn't twitch a hair. "What did black feet have right?"

"Those that lie down with dogs, get up with fleas," she said in a flat tone, her attention centered on the other side of the cabin. "And it's not black feet, it's Blackfoot."

Baffled by her response, he looked at the spot on the wall that held her attention – his humans had secured their framed copy of 'Rules for Non-pet owners who visit and like to complain about our cat' to Whispurring Winds' wall with enough Velcro to secure a dwarf. He'd ignored the foolish bit of antiqued paper since they'd installed it, but now wondered what Sharkey found so enthralling, so he read over the four points: 1) He lives here; you don't; 2) If you don't want fur on your clothes, stay off the furniture; 3) I like my cat better than I like most people; 4) To you he's an animal. To us, he is a son, who is short, hairy, walks on all fours and is speech challenged.

Xander winced at the last point. "I know it's insulting, but I let them keep it up to humor them."

"You think it's insulting to have your people put up a notice to the world that you're more important than other two-legs?" Her yowl hit such a high note that Mike's rhythmic snores stopped. "You-you-you – you have got to be the most self-centered guy I've ever met!"

"What's this?" Valentine asked from the cockpit, "A lover's quarrel."

"No!" they hissed as they turned in accord to glare at the their common enemy. Valentine's eyes showed thick halos of white as they advanced in unison, then he fled. For a moment, the urge to pursue him nearly overrode his sense of duty. With difficulty, Xander controlled the instinct. Sharkey, who wasn't as disciplined vaulted up the stairs, landed on a cushion, which slid across the cockpit like a runaway toboggan. She pitched sideways, smacking her head against the wheel.

He hurried onto the deck. "Are you okay?" She gave a short nod. Either she was still angry at him because of the stupid picture or she was too stubborn to admit getting hurt. He grabbed her head between his paws and checked her for injuries. "You're going to be sore for a few days," he said, as he inspected her left ear, "bruised but not broken." He sat down, waiting for her to say something … anything. The silence lengthened. He'd never met any female that could take silence – until now. "Still want to go with me?" She looked everywhere except at him. "Fine." He stood up to leave.

"Why did you call their tribute to you insulting?"

He paused. "I am not speech challenged – they are."

"So you think the whole thing is insulting just because they can't understand you?"

"No, just the part about being speech challenged, which is always the last thing I read and stays foremost in my mind."

She swallowed, her attention on the deck. "Maybe if you didn't read the last part, you'd realize how lucky you are." She glanced at him, her eyes shimmering. "I'd give anything if my people put up a sign that said I was more important than another two-legs."

Xander studied her as he digested what she had and had not said since he'd met her. "You haven't lived here your entire life, have you?" She stared at him, her eyes enormous with surprise. "And I'm willing to bet that you've lived on a boat at some point," he added.

"How did you know?"

"I wasn't totally certain until now." Her gaze narrowed. "You don't step on the lines, for one thing. Only someone that knew how treacherous they could be would know to avoid them." She gulped. "Is that the reason you're here? Did you step on a loose line and get pitched overboard?"

She shook her head. "I don't want to talk about this. Not here. Not now. Maybe when I know you better." Her voice trailed off as if she couldn't imagine anyone knowing her that long. She wiped her paw across her eyes, then added, "If you're still willing to have me, I'd like to come with you."

"Lead the way," he said in his normal voice, but as she moved past him, he whispered, "dogs are watching and I want them to think we're going to Kingston. We need to ditch them and head for the Blue Mountains." Sharkey gave an infinitesimal nod, then moved past as if he hadn't uttered a syllable. If the girl wasn't a spy, she was a credit to felinedom.

"Kingston is a rough place," she said as they walked

down the dock.

"Rougher than here?" He surreptitiously keyed 18 11'N 76 27'W, Whispurring Winds coordinates, into his collar.

"That's what I heard."

"Interesting." He dodged to his right, ducked under the stephanotis' fragrant white blooms, then eased through the wrought iron fence. Sharkey followed him, a baffled expression on her face. "No need to make it easier for the mutts than I have to." An 'oh' look flitted through her gaze, but he couldn't decide if she actually thought he was paranoid on the subject of canines – a possibility he'd mulled over on more than one occasion – or if she didn't fully understand how often a dog that appeared to be sound asleep was actually monitoring the movements of cats in his/her jurisdiction. According to his copy of Bartlebee's History, Opossum hunters had originally perfected the ability to 'hide in plain sight' and soon dogs of all types were lounging on porches and sidewalks all over the world as they spied on cats.

It was an effective surveillance technique; one that Xander practiced at every opportunity, too.

"I suppose you want to scare that rooster, or something so you have another excuse to climb another tree."

"You read my mind." Something few other cats ever managed to do. "The only problem is that this time of night, we'd have to climb a tree to find one." Sharkey might have the potential to be a purrtector. Perhaps even a top-notch one. If Simon proved to be nothing more than a translator for kitten stories and writer of inflammatory e-mail, which was all Xander could be certain of after their correspondence, he might recommend Ms. Sharkey for the Jamaican purrtector position. It wasn't on the level of being a continental purrtector, but it was a place to start.

Assuming she wasn't in league with the enemy, of course.

Again, he wondered what the island's cats had been thinking about when they nominated a scribe to be their defender.

Were Dame Esmeralda, Sharkey, Simon and Scalpy, the rough fellow who he'd noticed in a previous kickboxing tournament, the only cats in Jamaica?

"You weren't serious about us crossing the mountains to Kingston, were you?" Sharkey lowered her tone to a whisper then added, "They aren't all asleep, after all." That said, she casually set off toward a big red rooster, which was scratching away at the rock-hard soil under a streetlight.

He stopped her and motioned for her to simply climb the nearby tree. "No need to make him have a fit this time of night, it would only call attention to us." He followed her up the tree to the first broad branch. "Simon is meeting us at a coffee plantation in the Blue Mountains."

"Well, that's specific," she hissed. "Just how do you expect to find him? I've heard those mountains are really mountains. I've never seen them, but I hear that they're much bigger than the hills around here." Though she was halfway out on a branch, which intersected with another tree, she stopped, turned to face him and sat down on the limb.

Xander leaped over her and continued on without looking back. Either she got over whatever was bothering her, or not. He had a red claw situation to handle and while meeting Simon at some farm in the mountains might be a waste of time, it got him away from Valentine, Port Antonio and its roving packs of dogs, and most importantly, it would appear to the Purrsident and Council as if he was taking charge of the situation. Either way, he won. Now, all he had to do was get to the spot on Bowden road at the appointed time. He studied the miserable excuse of potholed asphalt, which his GPS unit confirmed was where the highway should be. Without signs, there was no way to confirm it was the correct road. He couldn't believe any country would have a main highway in such sorry shape much less that Bowden road was Port Antonio's main access to the Blue Mountains. He frowned as he recalled reading that it followed the Rio Grande between the Blue Mountains and the John Crow Mountains. Since there was no river in sight, it probably meant the human-made map was incorrect. Still, his cattonal GPS had never failed him and it stated this asphalt mess was the correct road.

Due to his confidence in Catamondo's technology, he hiked parallel with the road for two hours, but by the time dawn's rays illuminated his surroundings the vegetation had changing from somewhat civil to virtually impenetrable. Worse, even though the dense foliage provided excellent opportunities to conceal himself while he checked for followers it deterred forward progress. Clinging leaves combined with the humidity and increasingly vertical slopes made any progress extremely difficult. If he was late, the state of the island's infrastructure would provide a valid reason for whatever went wrong. He pressed on faster, then slipped downward. Xander's claws flashed out, grasping for a hold, but his slide increased to a blind plummet with damp leaves slapping his face and fur. Finally, one claw caught so hard he feared it would be yanked right out of his paw. He sank the other four claws into what felt like living wood, then maneuvered to find a purchase for his other paws.

The only solid spot in the muddy, moldy mire seemed to be the narrow area his right index claw had found. Once both front paws were secure and he caught his breath, he heard the sound of small, unseen feet scampering through the leaves; the high cry of a bird, speaking in a twitter he'd never heard; and the sinister sound of water playing among the cobbles of a shoreline.

Much as he hated to admit it, it was doubtful if he'd fallen victim to a trap laid by the dogs, something that would have been easier to deal with than one of Mother Nature's little geological surprises.

Should he move left, right or climb up the slimy root? He swayed sideways. The root started tearing. His only option became down. Not wanting to put off the inevitable until he was too tired to cope, he loosened his grip and plummeted through the thick, damp foliage. Abruptly he shot into the open, about six feet above the water and realized he was about to fall into the widest river he'd ever seen; he quickly grasped another root.

Years of training made his first reaction after avoiding disaster, a calming breath and his second a dispassionate assessment of his situation despite the strain on his claws and the dampness seeping through his fur.

A raindrop smacked his nose.

Hathor, what have I done to offend you?

Instead of an answer, cracks started ripping around his

claws. He adjusted his grip, but new fissures formed within moments of his shivs sinking in each new spot.

As he searched for a stable portion of the root, it started raining in earnest.

He'd never angered the goddess this badly! He peered upward, but the slick bank and leaves did not provide any escape. Sideways wasn't an option. That only gave him one alternative; he could take it now, or after he was too exhausted to plan a proper landing. Xander retracted his claws and plummeted toward the water. His paws smacked first, then his tummy and finally his chin. Then the water closed over him. He plunged several more feet, lungs burning, before contacting the rocky bottom. He leapt back toward the air. Moving through water seemed to take an eternity. Merlin frequently bragged about his daring feats in the water, so Xander knew moving through water with a strong current took longer. He just hadn't anticipated that he'd go deeper into river water than the ocean, which he'd become accustomed to.

His head finally broke the surface. He gasped in a lung full of air, then coughed up a mouth full of rain. Gasping, he paddled the way Merlin had taught him. It was impossible to see across the river, so he concentrated on the vertical side close to him, looking for anything, which could provide access to get back up the precipice. He marveled at the way so many trees had managed to hook their roots into the rock, but knew, from his embarrassing fall that those roots only provided the illusion of a retreat.

As the water propelled him downstream, he tried to swim across the river, but no matter how hard he paddled, he never seemed to get any further from where the cliff softened into a hillside. Finally, nearing exhaustion, he kicked toward a nearby rocky bank. It seemed like it took forever before he felt smooth stone beneath one paw. But after that first contact, he didn't touch bottom for several more feet. By the time he waded out of the river, Xander felt like he'd fought in five kick-boxing matches without getting a rest.

He hadn't been this soggy since he'd fallen in the Puget Sound. At least this water didn't smell as dirty as that had!

With his last ounce of energy, he shook the horrible water out of his fur, then, he flopped down in a dry spot and considered his alternatives. By the time the tips of his fur were dry, he'd concluded that the river was at least four times wider than the trees were tall, therefore his only way across the expanse of water was to either locate a kite so he could sail over or find a bridge. Since the former seemed unlikely, and because he knew it was impossible to swim across the horrid stream, he headed north, to find the bridge his map had shown.

At least the events of the day hadn't been witnessed by anyone.

By the time he fought his way through the dense undergrowth, it was nearly noon, but at least the rain had stopped. He leaped onto the road, grateful that his fur could finally dry in the open air, then he studied the metal bridge that looked a lot like what he'd seen kids build with tinker toys, except this thing was metal and had pavement, which shimmied and shook every time a car passed over it and shuddered like a quake when a bus or truck went over. Still, it offered a dry way across the darned river. He gauged the traffic, then sprinted during a lull, reaching the far side moments before a truck laden with green orbs thundered across. He sat down, exhausted.

"Hikes up into the forests are usually very rugged, river crossing, machete wielding, trailblazing affairs," a familiar voice said.

He turned to face Sharkey, who looked positively prim, dry and smug.

"How did you find me?" She looked at him, as if he'd asked the stupidest question on earth, and recalling the lack of roads, the river's current and the rugged terrain, it probably was the dumbest thing he ever had asked. "Forget I asked that. What do you know about this area?"

"This area is Jamaica's last remaining rainforest where many rare and exotic plants can be found as well as the world's second largest butterfly."

"Thank you for sharing that with me."

"This eastern face of the Blue Mountains receives more than 300 inches of rain each year, providing water for almost one half of Jamaica's population," she said.

"Did you memorize the country's data?"

"Yes." Her nose darkened.

He paused to look at her. "Why?"

"Because I learned useful stuff." He perked his ears, encouraging her to go on. She took the hint and added, "Like at Ginger House there is a pretty waterfall beside a cave and a mineral spring. A swinging bridge connects Ginger House to Cornwall Barracks." She grinned. "I've never had a dog chase me across it. And they say we are afraid of water."

Now that was interesting. "Where's Ginger House?"

"Near the marina."

"You'll have to show it to me when we return." She looked pleased. "How much farther is it to the coffee plantation?"

"Days by foot – maybe even weeks. But if we climb on top of the bridge and wait for just the right moment, we might be able to get there in a couple hours."

He studied the rusted girders. "You aren't talking about flying a kite there, are you?" She snickered and shook her head. "I was afraid of that."

"Look at it this way, you won't have to try to swim across the river again, and your fur will get blown dry."

"I'll look like a puff ball," he said, as he wondered how she'd known his fur was wet from swimming, not just the rain.

"You'll look handsome, just like always." She tilted her head. "Ready to climb? While I was waiting for you, I found a good place to wait for the perfect truck."

After the tree root and being saturated, the last thing on earth he wanted to do was climb an old rattletrap of a bridge just so he could leap off it and hopefully land on something survivable; of course, he was not about to admit that to her. "What are we waiting for?" He leaped to his feet and pranced a few steps. "Lead on." She checked for traffic, then sprinted toward the bridge, leaped high, landing on an angled girder and without pausing, dashed the rest of the way to the top. She hopped sideways, then stopped and looked back, apparently expecting him to be right on her pretty black tail. "Amazing," he muttered. Not to be outclassed, he copied her moves. When he was in midair, leaping toward the girder, the air felt suddenly hotter, and when his paws hit the old metal his pads burned like he'd hopped onto a stove – something he'd done once and vowed never to repeat. He clenched his jaw, focusing on balance and speed instead of his aching paws, and arrived on top of the structure in one flick of a tail. Since Sharkey had moved, he also copied her side-jump, which landed him on a shady, cooler, section of metal. Careful not to let his tail drape over the sunny area, he tried to appear casual and cool as if he was primarily interested in checking out the view.

"We need to be over here." She pointed at a wide, shaded girder on the other side of the bridge, but instead of moving, began licking her toasted toes.

Since that was precisely where he thought he should be and she was doing what he wanted to do, he joined her. "How'd you find this spot?"

"Did what you taught me, climbed the trees and surveyed the area, while I looked for something that could help us."

"You knew I'd come here."

"Only after Hector said your attempt to swim across the river failed." She turned toward him, her eyes huge with admiration. "Did you really do that, or was he telling me a whopper?"

"Who is Hector?"

"A heron I know."

Xander thought back to his miserable misadventure. "Blue, just a little taller than we are, skinny legs and neck?" She nodded. "And he's one of your spies." He couldn't have been more impressed.

"So you really, truly dove into the river and you know how

to swim!"

"Living on a boat, it seemed wise to learn." Suddenly, the entire bridge started to shake. "What in Hathor-" He spotted a decrepit bus rumbling across the bridge, its once-yellow paint faded and marred with rust and dents. Sharkey stood up. "Please tell me you don't plan to ride on top of that! The roof looks like we'd crash straight through." Worse, the metal top was probably scalding hot.

"Nope. I'm waiting for a produce truck, but my balance isn't as good as yours, so it's easier to stand up when things shake." She wrinkled her nose. "Preferably not pineapples or oranges, but we might not have a choice." He raised a brow. She sighed. "The produce truck will have a load. Pineapples are pokey and their leaves are sharp as kitten claws." Her nose turned dark pink. She was the blushingest gal he'd ever known. "Last time I jumped an orange load it wasn't pretty."

"Rolled on you, did they?" Gaze downcast, she nodded. "Worse things have happened to me." And more recently than he cared to admit. Lest he say more than he intended, he settled to soothing his aching paws. Hopefully, he wouldn't end up with blisters on his pads. After he'd done all he could, he worked on his claws, which were gummy with tree sap and grimy with caked mud. He should have ripped the bark off the disgusting tree for its insolence. His claws might not be in any better condition, but he'd certainly feel better. He peeked at Sharkey, who was also tending to her paws. Perhaps she was trying to impress him. If so, she was doing a darned good job of it.

Imagine having a heron for a spy and not even being the

Island's Purrtector. He peered at her, again. She hadn't been listed in his files, which wasn't unheard of, but a gal with her skills should have been listed somewhere. Perhaps Jamaica had lousy records. Or maybe the locals merely rated their cats by a different set of standards. He squinted at the clean claws on his left paw, then started manicuring the ones on his right. If Jamaican cats valued unusual skills, it would explain how Simon had been voted into office and why Sharkey frequently acted like she thought she was inferior. Another set of values would even explain why the local cats had allowed the dogs to take over Port Antonio.

Of course, if she was a spy for the dogs, that could also explain why she had drafted birds to answer to her. Worse, she would have had an opportunity to send information back to anyone she was associated with.

This port was turning into more of a problem than he would ever have believed possible. He finished his right paw and started cleaning mud and tree sap from his belly. Gradually, his thoughts calmed and the peace of being in a lovely shaded area, smelling the sweet scent of flowers brought by the gentle breeze and listening to the soft coo of birds while cleaning his pelt put him into a Zen state.

"I think this one will do," Sharkey called while he spruced up the fur on his left side. Her tail twitched with excitement as she assumed the pounce posture and waited for the vehicle to pass beneath. Grooming forgotten, he got into position beside her and timed the leap to land on the fluffy green heap in the back. The moment the truck cab rumbled past, he and Sharkey jumped with the precision humans generally attributed to the Blue Angel airplanes.

The smell hit a moment before they landed and he knew they'd made a mistake, but the only thing he had time to do was modify which feet he landed on. Even so, his rear paws sank through the topping of lettuce leaves and grass into the rotten fish beneath. The full force of the stench hit his nose a moment before he sensed something icky oozing between his freshly manicured toes. Sharkey landed up to her belly sending a shower of the Hathor-awful mess over him.

"I think we've found something worse than pineapples or oranges." It was difficult to speak while trying to hold his breath. Eyes watering, she merely nodded. He tilted an ear. "It might be better over there on those big leaves." At least they would be closer to the cab and presumably the motion of the truck could keep the worst of the smell behind them. Gingerly he extracted one paw, then took a tentative step. He didn't sink in as deep as he had with the added velocity of his leap. Carefully, he took one more step than another and another until he was on the relatively stable pile of foliage. He put his nose around the cab and inhaled deeply, then, feeling fortified, turned back to Sharkey, who had barely managed to move a third of the way. "Need help?" he asked, though he didn't have a clue what he could possibly do to assist her. She shook her head and determinedly took another step.

Darned if she didn't act like a Purrtector!

By the time she joined him, Xander had scraped most of the vile fish slime onto the huge leaves and was trying to figure out how to groom himself without actually licking his fur or worse, losing his kibble at the idea. When she finally staggered onto the leaves, Sharkey's nose looked white as the clean parts of her fur, "You'll feel better if you let the wind blow in your face for a while." She put her chin on the rail and closed her eyes. Her sides shuddered as she inhaled. Xander settled next to her, glad for the excuse to stick his nose back in the fresh breeze, while appearing companionable. "Feel better?" he asked. Her grunt could mean anything. "Pretty country," he said.

Sharkey turned her head and stared at him, her eyes brimming with tears. "Don't pretend to be nice to me. I know this mess is my fault. Cuss me out, throw me off the truck, do whatever, just quit being such a gentleman." She turned away, but not before he saw a tear trickle down her cheek.

What kind of background must she have to say such a thing? He scratched his ear before he recalled how filthy his rear paws still were. Hastily, he settled back down next to her. "No one has ever accused me of being a gentleman before." He scanned the rutted road ahead, then looked up at the sky. Not a rain cloud in sight and for once in his life, he would have welcomed a good shower. "You couldn't have known this truck was loaded with garbage and you certainly didn't push me off the bridge." She started crying in earnest. "Want to tell me about it?"

Sharkey shook her head. Patience being one of his strengths, Xander stayed quiet. After a long while she said, "When I was a baby, my humans got rid of me." It took all his willpower to appear relaxed, after all her story wasn't unique. He'd see 'free kittens' signs at every port of call. "I lived in the animal shelter for two weeks, then got lucky and was adopted." Her nose curled with disdain. Xander clamped his jaws shut to keep the questions inside, some deep part of him knowing that if he asked them, instead of let her tell her story in her own way, she'd keep it buried. "As soon as I was old enough, they stuck needles in me." Fresh tears flowed.

"That happens to a lot of us." The comment popped out before he could stop it.

"You, too?"

He nodded. "Whenever I hear the word 'vet' or see it written on the calendar, I disappear for a couple days." Hathor only knew what new torment the villainous veterinarian would perform the next time one of the sadists got him in their clutches! How many of his friends were missing claws? According to his files, even Simon was missing the ones on his front paws! And hadn't he met at least two cats, who were missing their tails? They hadn't been Manx, either. Humans often did insanely evil things to their owners in the name of fashion. Thankfully, the worst of the butchery seemed to happen to dogs, who frequently ended up with cropped tails, shortened ears and designer clothing. His whiskers twitched.

"What?" Sharkey asked.

"Remembering a Doberman I once knew." And had performed a nose-ectomy on. She looked at him expectantly. "Last time I saw Konan, a couple kids were pulling him down the sidewalk in their red wagon." He beamed at the memory of the tormentor of cats wearing a flowery, ruffled dress complete with matching vintage sunbonnet, which did little to hide his scared face.

"You broke his legs?" She looked at him as if he was the greatest cat on earth.

"I wish." He paused to watch movement in the road ahead of them. "Those don't move like cats or dogs."

"They're mongooses."

She had to be kidding. "I thought those lived in India."

"They probably do, but they're here, too. The good thing is that I haven't seen a snake since I came to this island."

He looked at the frolicking trio with renewed interest. Abruptly, one stiffened and looked down the road toward their truck. A moment later, all of them dashed into the underbrush. "They move a lot like cats."

"It's unusual to see them out during the daytime." Sharkey thought for a moment, the misery of her fur temporarily forgotten. "I haven't seen many in town, either."

"Ah, nocturnal forest dwellers. Nothing wrong with that." Nothing wrong with their obvious agility and joie de vivre, either. He wondered how mongooses – or were they called mongeese – felt about canines. If the dogs harassed them as badly as cats, they could be potential allies. As the old truck lumbered past the still-undulating undergrowth, he studied where the mongooses had vanished, but couldn't catch a glimpse of them. Their coloring is so similar to his own that they were probably naturals at concealment. Perhaps they're even some form of distant relatives. His whiskers twitched with the possibilities.

"What?" Sharkey demanded.

"You sure do ask a lot of questions." Jaw tight, she turned away from him. He immediately felt bad, so added, "Look, I'm sorry, I just have a lot on my mind right now."

"And I don't?" He looked at her slimy fur out of the corner of his eye and wished his wasn't in equally bad shape.

Xander inhaled. It was the worst thing he could have done. Eyes watering, lungs burning, he plunged his face back into the wind. "So, you are a feline, instead of some super-android cat," she said, her posture relaxing. "I was beginning to wonder."

He gasped for air until he felt safe trying to speak. "Why?"

Her tail made a nervous twitch. "Lots of stuff." He looked at her through a shimmering layer. "Okay, your eyes for starters." She took a quick breath. "I've never, ever seen any other cat with blue eyes. In fact, the only places I've ever seen that color in nature is in about 12 feet of Bahamian water or a Carolina blue sky. It's just not natural." Where had she been that she'd never seen another Siamese before? And how did she know that Bahamian water changed shade due to the depth? Obviously there was a lot more to Sharkey than his computer had revealed.

"When were you in the Carolinas?"

"Never."

"Then how do you know the sky there is the same color as some Bahamian water?"

"I've seen photographs," she snapped.

"So have I, but I never realized the colors were the same."

"I have an eye for color."

Obviously, and the ability was quite unexpected in such a cute black and white package.

She went on, "Most cats do not have eyes the color of water." Her eyes narrowed to slits of gold. "And they do not swim."

"If you say so." He studied her angry posture, which

seemed disproportionate to the topic. If they were going to work together on this case, he needed to know exactly who she was and what made her tick. "So, you've been to the Bahamas, probably arrived on a boat, since you seemed totally comfortable with Whispurring Winds' rocking motion, and you never learned how to swim. Very, very interesting, particularly coming from a girl who tells me her name is Shark Bait." He gave her his most sympathetic look. "Want to tell me about it?"

"No!" She turned her back to him and probably would have given a good performance of an outraged female if the truck hadn't suddenly made a sharp right turn and thrown her against him. His claws sank into the frond's fibrous shank as he held on for them both. A moment later, the truck straightened itself out, its tires grinding up a steep, rocky incline. Sharkey righted herself and peered ahead to see where they were going, just as the truck's brakes squealed and the driver jerked the wheel to the right. "It bounced off the road," she said, as if the problem wouldn't have been obvious to the dumbest dog. "But I don't think it's going terribly far – there's no road ahead."

The gears ground out an awful high-pitched note. A moment later, the truck lurched to a stop in front of a shabby shed, the crooked door burst open and two scantily-clothed brown children burst squealing from the dark interior. "Guess they figure if they make a big enough fuss with their welcome, their parents won't get mad about them playing in the tool shed." The dirt-smeared tikes waved, their thin arms like twigs sticking out of their tattered clothing. Xander looked from the children to the smiling couple getting out of the truck to the garbage beneath his paws. "You don't supposed they brought this mess home to eat, do you?" The children got so close he could see yellow snot dripping out of the smaller child's nose. A shiver ran down his spine at the thought of the nasty germs the humans and the rubbish might contain. "We gotta get out of here without being seen." Without waiting for her reply, he leaped over the back of the truck. He'd never landed on such steep terrain. Unable to secure any paws, he landed hard on his tail, then slid down hill amid an increasing cloud of dust and cascade of small rocks. Sharp things bruised his tail, but he didn't manage to stop his momentum until he splattered against a basketball size rock. As Sharkey plunged past him, he grabbed the scruff of her neck.

"Thanks," she gasped. She lay flat on the ground at his feet, either afraid to move or too stunned to budge. "You think they saw us?"

"Would it matter if they did?" She blinked, as if surprised by his comeback. "I didn't see any dogs."

"There are other enemies besides dogs."

"Yeah, the germs the little one had, come to mind ... I really can't afford to be sick right now." He studied her expression, baffled at why she seemed so angry, when his stomach was the one crushed against the rock, and sitting on a tail that was one huge aching 'carpet-burn'. "What's black and white and red all over?" He asked to take his mind off his pain. Her scowl deepened. "You covered with clay dust." He grinned at his own joke.

"Ha-ha. Very funny. You're a veritable Rolando." Sarcasm dripped through her disparaging tone.

"You don't like his brand of comedy?" She snorted. He looked around for an escape route – short of falling off the hillside. There wasn't an obvious option. He'd landed near a sturdy tree trunk; he studied its relatively smooth bark. Looks okay for climbing, but could he even stand up after the fall? There was only one way to find out. He looked farther upward into the low branches, which were armed with thick, sharp thorns. Climbing this tree with its big glob-like fruit would be a last resort. He looked back toward the humans, but they were walking toward the shed, so he continued his visual reconnaissance. If he hadn't slammed into the rock, he would have plummeted into the road. Xander's ears perked with interest at his suddenly expanding prospects. Again, he studied the tree's limbs, concentrating on the side jutting over the road. If nothing had been broken, sprained or maimed, his plan was possible. The only problem was that he could neither hear nor see a single vehicle on the road.

Sharkey said, "Do you think this smell will wash off?" She was staring at a glimmer between the trees on the far side of the road. Obviously, the map hadn't lied when it showed the road following the river until it was high in the mountains. "There's only one way to find out." Carefully he stood up and tested each limb as he gauged the leap onto the aged asphalt.

"You're serious!"

"As a dead fish." Specifically the one whose decomposing slime gummed his fur. "Come on." Everything except his poor tail seemed intact and soaking that in cool water would feel good. He leaped, landing safely on the warm, broken asphalt. There, he turned back waiting for her. Sharkey fidgeted. "It's easier than climbing that bridge and jumping off it. For one thing, you know where you're going to land and it's not burning hot." She hesitated. "Now!" he bellowed.

She jumped.

If circumstances forced him into the water twice in one day, he certainly didn't want to waste time contemplating the miserable prospect; he wanted it behind him and to be at a point when he could clean his poor fur, brush it and get groomed. He determinedly stalked across the road, then went down the steep bank on the other side without pausing. Fortunately, it wasn't as steep as the previous one, so he stomped across the sand straight into the water. He only stopped to examine his poor abused tail when he felt water rushing across his stomach. Xander stood in the disgusting water, hoping it would wash away the revolting slime and blood, while numbing the gravel-burn enough so he could retain his dignity in front of Sharkey.

There was a faint splash behind him. "I can not believe I'm doing this," she said.

Careful of the slippery rocks beneath his paws, he turned to her. "You only have to get the slimy parts."

"But the goo splattered e-v-e-r-y-w-h-e-r-e," she wailed. Xander narrowed his gaze, grateful for any distraction from his own sorry situation. "There are only a few gunky places on your side and back." Tears welled in her eyes, but she laid down in the water. "Will this really clean off the mess?"

"Hathor, but I hope so!" Sharkey moaned and turned her head away. Ripples expanded around her on the smooth surface of the water, as she shuddered. "I know it feels icky, but it's certainly better than worrying about getting asphyxiated breathing the stench or worse, having to lick off...." He dunked his head in the water and trembled at the thought of licking off his feet.

Stomach controlled for the moment, Xander resurfaced.

The poor girl looked like her dignity was propped on her last nerve. Since he didn't know what he could say that would make her feel better, and he didn't want to look at his tail, quite yet, he focused his attention on his rendezvous with Simon and what was turning into a Hathor-forsaken place to meet. His only solace was the thought that if the section of road from Kingston was anything like what they'd been over, Simon wouldn't have a pleasant journey, either. Xander wished he could use his collar to shoot off a quick e-mail, but knew better than to operate it in water.

Xander raised his right paw and studied his soggy fur. Was it his imagination or had the slow current washed away some of the mess? Ripples still encircled Sharkey's violently shaking body. "How you doing?"

"F-f-f-f-fish a-r-r-r-e e-e-eat-t-t-ting m-m-m-me."

This he had to see. Careful, so he wouldn't spook them, he went to her and peered into the water. A school of thin silvery fish no bigger than his paw clustered around the spots where he'd noticed globs of gunk, their tiny jaws working frantically. "I've heard of cleaner fish, but never seen them before."

"They aren't cleaner fish; bait fish, maybe."

How would she know? "Well, perhaps they aren't a normal cleaner fish, but that's what they're doing." He peered through the clear water. "They're pretty good at it, too. Just try to stand still." She clamped her eyes shut. Jaw trembling just above the water, she tried to stay still, but the more she fought her fear, the worse she shook. If Sharkey didn't manage to control her emotions, she could become the one-cat source of a tsunami in this river.

A few tiny fish moved toward him. Tiny jaws pulled at his

fur. Something nibbled the tender flesh of his backside. Xander started purring his favorite lullaby. Memories of his mother's beautiful voice and lavender flecked eyes washed over him. The moment he was dry, he'd send her a cyber card. He should do so more frequently than when the human calendar reminded him. Fortunately, since his mother was pedigreed, he had doZens of siblings, so she probably didn't miss hearing from him.

"You're right, they're cleaning the gook and leaving my fur and claws alone." Sharkey stared intently into the water. "I wonder what fish spit tastes like."

"Anything has to be better than what that slimy crap smelled like. It's a wonder I didn't asphyxiate the moment the stench hit my nose."

"By then, it was too late to avoid the mess." He nodded. "I really am sorry. I know it's totally my fault." She looked ready to drown herself.

"Worse things have happened," he said philosophically. The look she gave him shouted 'liar'. Xander sighed. "Yes, we're trashed, but it's for a good cause and fur does wash." He scowled. "You must promise me that you will never tell anyone that I voluntarily walked into this river."

"Or dove into it earlier?"

He felt his frown deepen. "You certainly do have an interesting spy network set up."

Her eyes widened with surprise. "Jorge is just someone I talk to."

"Right." Hadn't she said her bird-informant's name was Hector? And hadn't she referred to the seagull, who had monitored his arrival as Julio? "How many of your friends happen to have wings?" Her gaze dropped, confirming his suspicion. "Good story, but we all know that birds are only good for two things and information gathering is the use I like least." He licked his lips at the memory of the roast chicken they'd shared. Suddenly, it seemed like years since he'd eaten. He looked up as one of the odd blue birds flew over, skeletal legs trailing behind. His stomach growled.

"I have it on good authority that herons are mostly feather and bone." She held her chin high above the water, looking oddly dignified despite her body being submerged and surrounded by tiny feasting fish.

"Jorge's authority?"

"How'd you know?" He smiled at her naivety. Her gaze narrowed. "Oh... Well, nobody eats them, not even humans."

"It was simply a passing thought, but we should find something to eat – keep our strength up for the trip and all that." His stomach growled, again. "Did you see any chickens at that shack?" She shrugged. "We need to check it out. Where there are chickens, there are generally eggs – good eating and great for a shiny coat." He rippled his silken fur, then seeing Sharkey's morose expression, felt bad about forgetting her miserable state. As he tried to think of something nice to say, something bit him. "Ouch!" he howled as he leaped into attack pose.

"You okay?"

He nodded. Though he looked for his attacker, none was evident; still, he knew the phantom menace was close because he was missing a chunk of fur from his rear right leg.   He studied the area, finally noticing a rock that wasn't a rock. Hathor, why did you sic that turtle on me? How have I displeased you? "Watch out for turtles – they eat fur." Sharkey leaped straight up at least five feet high, then shot sideways and landed on the bank. If he hadn't seen it with his own eyes, he wouldn't have thought the jump was possible – particularly from a prone position and saturated with water. Imagine what that cute little gal could do if she were dry! Giving the turtle a wide berth, he walked out of the water. "Where'd you train?"

"Nowhere."

"I hope you don't expect me to believe that after the jump I just witnessed." He shook as much water as possible from his fur, so did Sharkey, who actually managed to look cute with everything but the top of her head saturated. He glanced down at his sodden legs, which looked positively ridiculous.

"It's the truth."

Xander rolled his eyes upward, but was too busy with his fur to argue.

"It is," she insisted. "If you must know, I lived on a Grand Banks. It's a kind of powerboat."

He paused with his grooming. "I've seen a few, but what does that have to do with how you learned to jump like that?"

"Well, I had to." The girl wasn't making a lick of sense, even though she was making startling progress on her fur. He stared at her until she paused to add, "I enjoyed dinghy bouncing when I was a kitten." She acted like that explained it all. He gestured with his tail for her to explain. "Dinghy bouncing is when your humans have at least two inflatable dinghies or at least there are two tied side by side to your boat." He gestured for her to continue. "Inflatable dinghies are nice and bouncy, like really cool big balls, but you know all about that because I saw that you have one. Did you know that you can walk on them without them rolling over?"

"Never tried," he admitted.

"Well, you can, and if you're good, you can bounce between two of them. It can be a challenge to time the jumps with the waves and stuff." Before he could request that she continue, again, she turned away from him and began to furiously clean her fur.

Several things were very clear to Xander: one) Sharkey had been very good at the game; two) she didn't like to talk about it, which meant that somehow bad memories were associated; three) that game sounded like it would be an excellent way to get exercise while living aboard Whispurring Winds and Hathor knew how difficult it was to keep his skills honed when he couldn't get to land.

He needed to motivate his humans to get a second dingy.

Chapter 6

"Gato escaldado del agua fría huye." A high-pitched voice said from overhead.

A scalded cat flees from cold water? Xander scanned the overhead boughs. Despite the fact that he didn't see another cat, he shouted, "For your information, neither of us was scalded." A twitter of avian laughter rustled through the leaves. He glanced at Sharkey, "So, you have one of your spies keeping an eye on us." His tail slashed.

"I do NOT have a spy network." She flattened her ears and narrowed her lovely golden eyes at the treetop. "As far as I know, dogs don't climb trees, so I guess I can't blame them." Then, she narrowed her gaze at him, adding, "And for your information, I don't speak whatever language that was, so since YOU understood whatever was said, and YOU apparently believe in spies, I'd probably be correct in suspecting YOU of having something watching us."

Did she need to shout? "I think it was Spanish, I don't actually speak it," he said softly, hoping she'd calm down.

"Yet you translated it."

"I've studied Latin, and that gives me a clue to other Romance Languages … it could have been Italian or

Portuguese, but Spanish is the most likely."

"I speaka de Eng-leash," a long-necked, spindly-legged, white bird said as it fluttered from the tree toward the water. As its long legs disappeared below the surface, its neck curved into an S and it tucked its glistening white wings tight against its body. Xander wondered if the body language meant the odd looking thing was considering unspoken questions, or if cats were the only ones that punctuated such thoughts with body language. "You, wid de azul eyes." Xander's ears perked. "Si, you. Eff you want de informa-sion I haf been instructed to gib, you will not eben think of eating me. Comprende?" Xander nodded. "Bueno." "An' you?" The bird's beady black gaze darted to Sharkey. She nodded, too. Satisfied with their answers, the bird's head disappeared beneath the water's surface. But before either cat had a chance to react, the bird popped back up, a silvery fish grasped in its long beak. Xander watched in fascination as the bird's neck made a sinuous movement and the fish disappeared.

Since he was sopping wet, he didn't dare try to use any of his collar's functions. "No one will ever believe this and I can't record today's events in my journal," he muttered. Fortunately, there was no record of either dunking in the river or the reason why the second time had been voluntary.

Sharkey looked at him, "Each bird loves to hear himself sing."

"Of course they do," Xander said, "What's that got to do with this situation?"

"I don't know, but that Arapaho saying came to mind and then popped out my mouth."

Xander blinked, and wondered where this strange little gal had ever heard such a thing, but that wasn't the main issue at the moment. With as much dignity as he could muster in his sodden state, he turned back to the bird. "You indicated that you had a message for us."

"You, si, he did not tell me you wid a senorita."

"He, who?"

"El Maestro-"

"And he is?" But the bird ignored him and just kept talking.

"- say 'fly ahead y le'bet you know found indicio'." The heron flapped his wings to emphasize the exciting statement. "Y he probable late."

"Are you talking about Simon?" Xander demanded.

"Si, si, El Maestro." With a glistening shower of droplets, the bird headed skyward.

"Well, I'll be," Xander muttered.

"What? You've never seen a heron fly before?"

"Certainly," He watched the odd bird fly due West, "I've never had anyone send a message by one, though." He scowled, "It's not like pigeons or something one considers to be a messenger." Just how many messenger herons did Simon employ? The fact that he could send messages to cats under his purrtection, regardless of their access to technology helped Xander understand why Simon had been elected to a post, which his training probably had not prepared him for.

Sharkey's nose wrinkled. "Pigeons are nasty birds. They'll poop on you just for fun." She raised her chin and looked him in the eye. "The herons I've met are nice. And

I've never seen one stupid enough to fly straight into a window or known one malicious enough to poop on a cat for sport."

"You've heard of some that fly into windows?" She looked at him as if he'd asked the dumbest question she'd ever heard. Not having had the opportunity to meet many pigeons, he admitted, "I thought peregrine falcons were the only ones dumb enough to do that."

"Aren't they extinct?"

He twitched his ear to indicate a negative. "Not yet. Before I moved my people aboard my boat..." His thoughts swirled away, as he recalled the dastardly way his humans had drugged him with catnip and while he was unconsciousness, moved him aboard the boat, all without the consideration of asking him. He inhaled deeply at the memory of their presumption. Their timing could not have been worse. Still, everything had ultimately turned out well. Nonetheless, he still missed his lovely yard, the entertainment offered by the bird-feeder and the gossip shared by the squirrels.

"Before you moved your people aboard your boat, what?" she asked.

"Sorry, I got lost in memories for a moment. As I was saying, I met a peregrine, who flew into my window and knocked himself out. I thought he'd killed himself and was getting ready to claim his body. Bird is my favorite food, after all." Xander scratched his ear. "But then, the bird sat up, and shook his head. His balance seemed off, but he grabbed the cardinal, that he'd been chasing – that one had a broken neck – and left."

"So," Sharkey said, "the falcon chased a cardinal into the window." Xander nodded. "The falcon survived, but the other didn't."

Xander nodded, again. "Now that I'm thinking about it, peregrines might not be dumb." He stared at the distant heron as he recalled how frequently the falcon had chased smaller birds into that same window after that, but he'd never collided with it, again. Obviously birds, at least herons, could be far smarter than they appeared, they could also find their way through clouds far better than anyone seeing them dither in the water would suspect.

Something growled. Before thinking, Xander leaped into defensive posture and found himself facing Sharkey. Her eyes widened for a moment prior to her gaze dropping. "Sorry," she muttered in a barely audible tone, "my stomach always does that when I'm hungry."

The fur on his back settled as he looked around the desolate area. "Mine does, too," he admitted. "Do you know if there are any restaurants around here?" She shrugged, confirming that she was as baffled by the area as he was. "I guess our best bet is to move back up to that shed and see if there's anything edible there."

"That's a human house, not a shed." He squinted through the foliage at the dilapidated structure that looked more like the derelict outhouse he'd once seen than anything the humans he knew would consider home. Sharkey snickered. "Sir Xander, we're not in the States anymore. Trust me, it really is a human house." As if confirming her statement, a small naked child scurried out of the distant door, it's skin several shades darker than the barren ground. A chicken squawked and at least two dogs barked.

Xander's ears perked up. "Where there's a chicken, there are often eggs, and if not, there's still the chicken."

"Those people probably need the food more than us."

"Which is why we try for eggs first."

"As long as we aren't after fish," she grumbled.

"I know what you mean." He led the way staying upwind of the truck and its foul cargo.

Chapter 7

The sun's burning rays dropped beyond the rugged, haze-shrouded mountains. For several minutes, the sky flashed orange, gold and red, then abruptly all color vanished. Shocked by the suddenness of the sunset's abrupt demise, Xander's claws sank into the tree limb, which stretched over the now concealed road.

"We'll be able to see a vehicle coming for a long way," Sharkey said, stating the obvious, as a thin beam of light glistened off the distant hillside. "Of course, the way they adjust the darned headlights, they could blind us up here instead of bathe the road."

"In which case, the vehicle will probably end up at the bottom of a gully, so we should avoid hopping a ride on it." He studied the seemingly erratic progress of the approaching vehicle as it slowly proceeded in their direction, headlights bouncing up and down, other times swaying from side to side as it passed along the curving, rutted road.

Assuming it was a truck, or some other type of vehicle they could hop onto, they would need good night vision to time their jumps and landings. He turned away from the intriguing light, controlled his breathing and relaxed as his eyes adjusted to the darkness, then hearing rustling near the base of their tree, he perked his ears in that direction trying to analyze the unfamiliar nighttime sound. Before he could, there was a crackle beyond the road followed by the crunch of something heavy landing on dirt. Xander's fur rose to attention as he tried to monitor all directions. Unfamiliar reddish-gold eyes glinted in the darkness. He flexed his claws, preparing for everything, except the unseen insect that bit his ear.

"Ouch," Sharkey said amidst a sudden flurry of movement.

Xander swiftly turned to help her, but couldn't see why she was flailing around. "Are you under attack?" Three more stings peppered his tender ear.

"I thought we'd be high enough up here, but the no-see-ums found us, anyway."

"Gads, how can they bite so hard when I can't even see them?"

"I think they're half crocodile."

"Sure feels like it." He thought a moment, then asked, "That wasn't one of your quotes, was it."

"No, but since you like them, 'Ea Nigada Qusdi Idadadvhn.' Seems appropriate. It's Cherokee for 'All my relations in creation', but I gotta tell you that I'm not too pleased to call certain creatures my relations." Her words were punctuated with bursts of activity as she battled the unseen cloud of vampire-insects.

"I don't think I want to call them kin, either." He smacked one on his ear so hard that he nearly knocked himself off the branch. "I don't suppose you know a more effective way to deal with these demons?"

"If I did, I would be doing it instead of getting eaten alive.

Of course, the Lumbee say, 'Seek wisdom, not knowledge. Knowledge is of the past, Wisdom is of the future'."

"In that case, perhaps we need to get out of this tree so fast they can't follow."

"They're awful fast, how could we do that?"

"By jumping another ride. There weren't any bugs on that rotten fish and any other time I've seen that sort of garbage, it's been covered with flies and bugs."

"True, but what are our chances of those headlights belonging to a truck?"

"Fifty-fifty." He closed his eyes, willing his senses to prepare for the noisy vehicle's arrival. "Perhaps it's a tractor pulling a wagon. The tractors I've encountered sound loud like that."

"Sounds like a motorcycle to me."

"True." He blindly batted at the voracious insects. "But I'm feeling lucky today; how about you?"

"Don't ask me that question right now."

"Good point." He lifted one lid a fraction so he could determine how far away the loud transportation was. "Wonder if that thing ever had a muffler."

"And I wonder which is the worse situation, being eaten alive or going deaf when we're only half eaten."

She had a valid point, if the thing edging around the curve a half mile away was already so loud that the entire tree seemed to shake, how bad would it be up close? "The good news is that it looks like a pickup truck."

"And the bad news?"

"That it's the loudest one I've ever seen."

"Or heard. I figured you were going to say something about not being able to see where to land and if you had, I'd have quoted my favorite Zuni saying, 'After dark all cats are leopards'."

"Well, Ms. Leopard, are you ready for another leap of faith?"

"As ready as I'll ever be. After all, nothing can be as bad as that last one."

"True. On the count of three. One. Two. Three." They leaped through the cloud of insects, landing on the corrugated surface of the empty truck bed. He inhaled with relief and smelled the pungent aroma of coffee. "At least this truck smells okay."

With a sigh, which could have either been relief or resignation, Sharkey sat down and began to groom herself. Suspecting that both conversation and sleep would be impossible in such a din, Xander did likewise, once his fur was laid neatly in place, he stretched out on the corrugated surface, closed his eyes and focused on finding a solution to Dame Esmeralda's catnapping.

During the dark, bumpy journey the ride became hypnotic and he slept, only to waken when the truck jolted to a halt. He put his nose close to Sharkey's ear and whispered, "Rise and shine." Her golden eyes popped open. For a fleeting moment, her attention centered on him, then it shifted to something behind him and a look of horror engulfed her features. "Dear Hathor, its head is about to explode!" As black eclipsed the golden flecks in her eyes and the white expanded, Xander tried to appear calm while turning to face the unseen danger. The truck shuddered as the faded red door screeched opened. His fur stood on end, as he spotted a gigantic emerald and gold head emerging from the cab.

Dear Hathor, what demonic entity had consumed the driver while he slept?

"Do you think it knows we're here?" Sharkey whispered.

He batted an ear, his attention fixed on the unknown horror. Someone called out a 'halllooo' and the thing lifted its long, black bony appendage and waved. Without turning to look at the back of the pickup, the thing slammed the door shut and briskly moved away. Only when it was clear of the truck did Xander dare turn his attention to the surrounding area and look for other dangers.

"Are those black things falling off the top snakes?" Sharkey's voice crackled with fear.

He swallowed, "I don't see any eyes." He peered at the thick, black things merrily swaying over the monster's red-satin back. "Of course, those could be tails." Sharkey moaned. "Or not." For a second, he thought she was going to slap him. "They almost look like the globs of fur Jessica used to get. She was a collie," he added, so Sharkey wouldn't think he knew any cats who were so lazy that they got fur balls. She was silent for so long, that he finally turned his attention from the retreating snake-thing to her.

Golden gaze unblinking, she studied the creature, but to her credit, she appeared more interested than terrified. "Puppies," she murmured.

Sure enough, seven of the fat brown beasts bounced out of the two-story concrete building to welcome the snake-head-demon. "Trust dogs to consort with something like that."

"I've never seen one with such a big head, but I think it's a rasta. At least it smells like one."

"What kind of devil is a rasta?"

She looked surprised. "Rasta is short for rastaman, like the one that you saw on the bamboo raft in the harbor."

He studied the thing as it went inside the building. "It does have the same nasty smell as that other one." He frowned. "What, exactly, are rastas?" When she appeared confused by his question, he added, "Human?"

"As far as I know." She glanced at the building. "Lots of people look different, though that one is the most different one that I've ever seen."

"Have you ever seen one with a cat?" She shook her head in a negative way. "I didn't think any of us would adopt such an evil thing, but it worries me that the dogs have." It took a second to realize he'd stated the thought aloud.

When the last puppy scampered into the dark interior, he motioned for Sharkey to follow him, then without waiting he leaped over the far side of the truck's railing, dashed across the open expanse of broken asphalt and into the welcome shelter of a big plant with large, long, fragrant trumpet-shaped flowers. He whirled as soon as he was deep in the shadows and looked to see if any of the canines were following. None were, so for the moment, he could relax, figure out precisely where they were and make a plan to meet Simon. Xander tapped his collar, then listened to the soft tones that conveyed his location. He grinned. "We're really close to the meeting site." Sharkey, who was peering through a plant covered in vibrant pink blossoms, didn't respond. "See anything of interest?"

"Breakfast, at least I think it could be." His stomach rumbled so loud it startled both of them. She gave him a halfhearted smile. "I guess that grass didn't fill you up, either." She twitched her tail to indicate a nearby wooden building. "Have you ever heard of humans hanging fish on a laundry line?" He eased next to her, shoulders touching as they studied what must be the monster's mate, as it hung doZens of beheaded, gutted and split fish tail-high on a dingy plastic cord that zigzagged across the dismal dirt yard. "Are those things fish?"

"I think so, but I've never heard of anyone hanging them like laundry. You don't think they're some sort of clothes, do you? I mean, I've seen some fabric that was painted like water, and some like leaves, but I've never seen anything quite like that."

"It's putting them up one at a time," he pointed out, as the entity clipped another pin over another tail. "We'll get one when – are rastas both male and female?"

"The only ones I've ever seen have been male." She frowned as she, too, studied the stringy, matted hair hanging well past the obviously female hips. "Aside from the hair, she almost looks like a normal woman."

"I wonder if all humans in these mountains stink."

"The rastamen I've encountered don't bathe, being smelly is like some sort of religion with them."

"That could certainly account for some of the odor." His whiskers twirled as he studied the line's path and the potential fish he could grab. "Of course, part of the aroma could be those fish. Thank goodness they generally taste okay." The woman took another fish out of the basket made of thin, woven branches and added it to the half-full line. Strange that all the fish seemed to be the same type and size. When Mike and Ginny fished, they rarely caught two alike in the same day, much less dozens. Of course, his humans were just as likely to catch a shark, which created all sorts of chaos on the deck, so perhaps the rail-thin woman with the loose-fitting yellow and green dress was smart to catch the same type.

He'd never truly understood why his humans hung clothes up to dry – of course he'd never fully understood their obsession with clothing to begin with – but the logic behind hanging fish out to dry totally eluded him. He said as much to Sharkey, who theorized, "Maybe drying them isn't really the goal. Maybe they're bait for something else."

"Like what?"

"Maybe a bird … perhaps a vulture?"

"Why would humans want to catch them, and how would they catch them? Those are normal clothes pins, not hooks."

"For that matter, where are the heads?" She sighed. "Look, I really don't know anything, I'm just trying to think of alternatives, because I can't figure out why any sensible person would want to hang perfectly good fish out to dry. I mean, why did they go through all the trouble of cleaning them, just to ruin the best parts? It simply does not make sense."

Xander agreed, but then very little had seemed logical since he'd arrived at this odd island.

By the time the strange woman went inside the concrete

structure, the first fish had begun to turn a dull gray. "I'm going for the last two she hung up," he said. "I'll knock off the pins, you catch them as they fall then dash into the shrubs on the other side. If either of the dogs gives chase, I'll deal with them, you just focus on getting away."

"Where should I go? Those bushes won't keep dogs out for long."

"Where would you be comfortable running to with a fish or two?"

"They don't look too heavy, I mean the line doesn't sag under their weight, and they're shorter than me, so I guess, if they aren't too slippery, I could get up a tree, but it would be easier if it had low branches." She studied the ones beyond the yard.

"That grapefruit tree looks good."

"Isn't it too close?" She frowned. "Citrus usually have thorns, but those should be more of a problem to dogs than me. At least I hope so."

"It's probably close enough." Anything farther would surely cause her to drop their breakfast. "Do you think you could make it to the lowest branch with one fish, then pause a moment?" She nodded. "Good, then when the dogs start howling at the base of it, drop the fish."

"This is your plan?"

"Yes."

"Why?"

"Do you know how dogs like to fight over bones?"

She snorted. "Of course."

"Don't you think they'd fight over a fish the same way?"

"Oh!"

"So, you figured it out?"

"Yes, I get them to follow me to the tree, when they think they have me cornered, I drop the fish. They fight over the fish and forget about me, so then I change trees and get away."

"That's it, exactly."

"But what about our breakfast, if I have to give it to them?"

"Simple, once the dogs are fighting over the fish you drop and are no longer paying attention, to either of us, I grab a couple more and meet you in the bows of that breadfruit tree." He pointed his ear.

He studied the dismal yard, planning his route and deciding how to misdirect the disgusting dogs. "Ready?" She indicated that she was. "On the count of three." His muscles quivered with anticipation through the quick countdown, then they were off across the barren yard. A dog yelped in alarm, but it was too far away to interfere. Before it could scramble to its paws, he leaped for the line, grasping it the way he'd seen gymnasts do with one paw and batting off pins with his other. One, two, three, four .... the fish plummeted toward the ground.

Though he'd only expected Sharkey to catch one, she caught the first two and the last one. When she moved to grab the third from the ground, he shouted, "Leave it. Run!" She disappeared under the bush before he hit the ground.

An ugly brown dog barreled across the yard, dust flying as its paws hit, barks of murderous rage spewing and eerie yellow eves murderous. Hathor. but he hadn't expected it to be quite so fast, but his plan still looked viable. After pausing to grab the last fish, he doubled back toward the plant with big, pale trumpet flowers, the dog was so close to his tail, that he was certain he could feel its hot breath. As soon as he was under the bush, he dropped the fish, expecting the stupid dog to be distracted by it. It wasn't. The beast obviously wanted him, period. But that wouldn't happen easily. Xander dodged around the trumpet flower's thick stalk and changed course, always leading the dog away from Sharkey, giving her time to get their food to safety. The first dog was joined by the second, then a third he hadn't noticed. Where had it come from? He didn't have time to analyze the answer, only time to react. Xander dodged under a decaying wooden structure. The sudden dark nearly disorienting him. The overwhelming stench of dog nearly overpowering him. Four pairs of yellow eyes stared at him as the first dog dived toward his tail. With an expert move, he kicked backward, his claws sinking into tender nose.

A new sort of howl rent the air, but he didn't stop to savor the moment, he headed straight at the dogs who'd been too lazy to join the chase. Kicking and scratching, and doing what he did best, Xander slashed through the inept mutts. Soon, the howls of pain sounded loud enough to shake the flimsy structure's entire foundation.

"Whad you do-in dow dare?" A furious male voice bellowed from overhead. "Ge out heh, now!" A kick at an unprotected ear caused a shriek. "Donnut mak me cum unda dare!"

Xander landed a few more easy kicks, then squeezed through an opening filled with dusty spider webs. Without pausing to look back, he dashed around the concrete building and leaped into a tree well away from Sharkey's. Only when he was halfway up and the stupid dogs still hadn't come after him, did he take the time to pause on a broad branch and clean off the cloying webs. "You missed one."

"What are you doing here?" he demanded. "You're supposed to be up the grapefruit tree."

"The fish are." He looked around. "I did what you taught me to do, I took the squirrel route, but only after it was obvious that you'd dumped them. What did you do to those nasty dogs, anyway?" He shrugged. "I've never heard such a racket, ever. Especially after that fish-lady came out and started beating the dogs with her broom." Sharkey laughed. "That's when I decided it'd be safe to come over here and see why you were staying here."

Xander grinned. "I hoped that if we left one of the fish, they'd get the blame."

Her eyes glinted with understanding. "The Oklahoma Indians say, 'A starving man will eat with the wolf'."

"You mean those monsters got down in the dirt to fight over the fish?"

"Not that I noticed, and I was watching." She looked him over, noting the globs of web he'd wiped on the truck, then her gaze crept upward. Her eyes widened with concern. "Oh, my gosh, you're bleeding!"

"Where?" She grasped his head between her forepaws and licked his ear. It felt delightful, so whatever he'd nicked it with, couldn't be too bad. "Are you sure it's my blood?" he asked.

Sharkey gagged. "No. ...Yes. ...Uh, Hathor, how can I tell?"

Chapter 8

Moments before the sun dipped behind the cloud-shrouded mountains, Sharkey tapped Xander's shoulder and whispered, "I hear someone coming."

Instantly awake, he maneuvered to the vantage point they'd discovered overlooking the meeting site, which was no more than a wide spot of a jungle trail. He peered through the shadows, but the sounds and voices were coming from beyond the rocky spit of mountain. "Azul eyes, no comprende de linga ou des montanas, so we probable wait."

"Not bloody likely," Xander sniffed.

"I wonder if that's the same bird he sent earlier, or if everyone in Kingston speaks that odd language," Sharkey whispered. Not having a clue as to the correct answer, Xander remained silent.

"Zee chica Azul es wid es bella, perhaps they find a casa for de coochiecoo."

Sharkey's nose, the barometer of her emotions, flamed bright red. Xander chuckled softly, then leaned close to her ear and spoke quietly, "You gotta give the bird credit for having one thing correct, you are beautiful."

She shook her head. "The Assiniboine say, 'Most of us do not look as handsome to others as we do to ourselves.' "

Interesting how she always quoted some Indian tribe when she felt embarrassed. "Find a mirror and take a good look, then realize that those sayings you keep quoting are only half correct – in this case, I think you really mean that you don't think you're as attractive as everyone else thinks." When her embarrassment deepened, he switched the subject, "How do you want to handle this, climb down the tree and be obviously waiting for them or stay up here until they're certain they got here first?"

"That bird acts like I'm invisible."

"What do you mean?"

"Just what I said, he acts like I'm invisible … Did you notice that you were the only one he spoke to?"

"I thought that was because Simon sent him to find me, I didn't realize you'd felt ignored." His perspective seemed to mollify her. "So, how do you want to handle the meeting?"

"Do you have a preference?" she asked as a heron and an earth-toned long-hair cat strolled around the boulder,

"No," he said in a normal tone, as he stood up.

The bird looked up at the branch they were on, squawked and shouted, "Hallllo, Azul Eyes! Zoo bind de right place! Good cat!"

"If that blasted bird keeps up the noise, heron will be on today's menu," he growled, so only Sharkey could hear.

She snickered. "Even if the feathered one is your friend's friend?" He gave a decisive nod. Sharkey snorted and shook her head. "He sure has good eyes."

"True," Xander said, then he leaped down from the

branch. "Morning," he said as he landed gracefully in the center of the path. Once on ground level, he was surprised to learn how tall and bulky Simon appeared. Either the kid had grown since he'd been elected, last autumn, or the long hair hid skin and bones. Or perhaps the data in his file was wrong, because the only thing about the cat coming toward him that matched his data was the friendly grin and breed. "Pleased to meet you." Xander stepped forward and rubbed cheeks with the tom, who stood at least two inches taller than him at the shoulder and, except for being a Maine Coon, appeared to be similar in size to his best pal, Merlin. Despite the fact that his profile didn't show a background in the martial arts or tournament trophies, the boy had good muscle tone and that didn't come from sitting in front of a computer all day long, while he wrote kitten tales.

"Glad to see you made it safely." Simon's voice was a pleasant mix of the normal Maine Coon twitter coupled with an Old World British accent and a bit of island spice. Xander bet the ladies loved him and judging from the way Sharkey was looking at him from the tree branch, his guess was correct.

"Pleased to finally meet you," Xander said.

"I know you've met Tango, but who is your lovely companion?"

"Ms. Sharkey, presently of Port Antonio, has been kind enough to be my guide." Knowing she'd be blushing all over her nose over being called lovely, he turned his attention to the bizarre bird. "Tango is an interesting name, how did you come by it?"

'Lik dis." Despite the big floppy wings and long spindly legs, or perhaps because of them, the heron launched into an intricate series of dance steps, ending with a wing swept low in an elaborate bow.

"I'm impressed," Xander said truthfully, though he was much more impressed with the way Simon had managed to tame the creature into becoming his messenger. He turned his head toward Simon, "Anything new on Dame Esmeralda's situation?"

"Other than the ransom?"

"You've never mentioned one previously." Xander's paw itched to slap the silly boy for overlooking such a crucial bit of information.

"The family received it, yesterday. That's what detained me." Xander motioned for him to go on. "It only listed an amount – one million euros – in cash, payable at a time and place of their choosing. The family has one week to come up with the money."

Xander tried to recall how much a euro was compared to a dollar. The last he'd checked, one US dollar equaled over one-hundred Jamaican dollars, so it was difficult to tell what the actual amount requested might be. "Why in euros?"

"I imagine because of their stability and universality compared to our own island currency."

"Are euros common here?"

"Only when a cruise ship docks for the day, otherwise, not... I'm speaking for what I see in Kingston, when the ships come in." His tail swished. "That is where the catnapping seems to have begun," he explained. "Then I followed the clues to an inland tour that visited places like the coffee plantation just the other side of this mountain. My friends," Simon glanced sidewise at Tango, "tell me that one of the families on the tour dropped out, when they got there."

"And you believe this has something to do with Dame Esmeralda?"

"It is possible." His tail made a frustrate swish. "If this family was part of the catnapping, the situation is more widespread than I assumed." He sat down and made himself comfortable by wrapping a tail, which was fluffy as a feather duster over his toes. "If I'm wrong, then I have been following the wrong leads for days, but I think I followed the correct ones. Dame Esmeralda's humans are more familiar with euro currency since they travel there, frequently, but I could not locate them to ask about this."

"So, they aren't like people from the United States, who use plastic cards to cover all types of currency?"

"Maestro, somwon come."

Both cats turned in tandem to meet the potential threat. Xander sniffed the breeze, catching the vague scent of at least one unwashed dog and something totally unfamiliar.

"Peppy, is that you?" Simon asked. A black nose appeared in the grass, quickly followed by a long tan nose, dark beady eyes and a thick neck. Then, the animal stopped, it's body hidden by foliage and shadows... Xander wondered what it was hiding. "Come out, my friend," Simon urged. The odd creature took another step forward on dainty paws, then muscular shoulders emerged from the tall grass. But the rest of it's body remained masked by the thick plants bordering the path. "You know Tango," Simon told the fellow with the black nose, "so let me introduce you to Sir Xander, my superior and his lovely friend Ms. Sharkey who seems as timid as you, since you won't come out of the underbrush and she won't come out of that tree."

Sharkey landed so close to Xander that he felt the earth quiver. Ignoring the short-legged, long-nosed gent, she addressed Simon, ""The Omaha say 'It is easy to be brave from a distance' and I'm sure they're correct, but it's also polite to keep a distance when others have business to attend to." She gave Tango a superior look.

Simon laughed. "Bravo, but somehow I suspect that you wouldn't be here if Sir Xander didn't consider you an ally." He raised a questioning brow. Xander indicated agreement. "So, you as well as my own companions really should feel included in the discussion."

"I have never had or considered having a serious talk which included a ferret and a heron." Though she tried to conceal her distrust, the way Sharkey watched Simon's companions left little doubt about her opinion.

"I am not a ferret," Peppy said, but she ignored him.

"Up until a year ago, I would have shared your opinion," Simon said.

"I am not a ferret," Peppy repeated.

"Then these two literally saved my life and I learned that best friends could come in all shapes, sizes, colors and types."

"Do I look like a ferret?" Peppy asked from Xander's side. He flinched. The creature had moved so silently that he hadn't had a clue. And that was something that had never happened to him before arriving in Jamaica. "Well, do I?"

To cover his distress over his lack of awareness, Xander made a production of turning and studying Peppy's strange body. Though he appeared normal on front, his tail looked almost like a crocodile's – wide where it connected to the body, tapering down to a tip.

"I've only met one ferret," Xander said truthfully, "it was white and had a small tail, but there are a few similarities in your face structure." Peppy sniffed with depreciation, though Xander didn't know if it meant the creature was insulted by his comment or that the sound was typical of whatever animal he was. "If you aren't some relative of ferrets, what are you?" Peppy's jaw clamped into an angry line. "I only ask because I want to understand. I've only been on this island a few days, and you're the first of your kind that I've met."

"I am a mongoose."

"He es a primo de un fee-rat."

"How would you like to dance your fancy steps with one leg?" Peppy snapped. Tango twirled away, chortling as if it was a routine threat.

"Well," said Xander, "I know Ms. Sharkey never intended to insult you." He glanced at her in time to see her looking up at Simon as if he was better than catnip. "As I understand it, you and the bird are Sir Simon's chief aids-"

"Friends. We are friends, nothing more," Peppy interrupted.

"Well, I don't have many friends that would hike all the way into these mountains with me, and any I do have, I consider very trusted friends, and perhaps even chief aids. So, perhaps we have a slight language problem, because I consider aids a very honorable position."

"Simon said you were very good at politics. I see he was

correct," Peppy said.

"Do mongooses often have bird and cat friends?" Xander asked.

"Other countries, perhaps not, but here, El Maestro listens and we share a common enemy."

"The dogs."

"Yes."

"I understand why you became allies, but not why you were willing to hike this far for a catnapping."

"But Ms. Esmeralda is not just any cat, is she?" Peppy asked. "If Tango and I help with this, and we rescue her, then we have a better chance that your society will help us."

"What do you want?" Xander asked.

"They want what they have always wanted," Simon said. "To be heard and understood."

Peppy nodded. "This is what everyone want."

Tango beat his wings in disagreement. "Es no true! De dogs, zay vant be roi. Y rule eberyvan."

Xander was inclined to agree with the bird's view of dogs wanting to dominate, so moved a bit closer to him, but not so close that an excited movement of the wings would touch him. "What we really need is good, up to date information." He looked at Simon. "Do you have anything new? The last I've heard is two days old."

Sharkey snorted. "Like you've been in a situation so you could get anything." She batted her ears toward the encroaching jungle. "Half the time, we haven't even known where we were."

Simon glanced at Xander't throat, eyes got wide, then he started blinking rapidly. "Seriously?"

"Of course." She sat up tall and proud. "It's a wonder we actually managed to meet you at the right place and time." She turned her attention to Tango. "Your feathered friend is the only contact we've had since leaving Port Antonio."

Simon blinked several times, then turned toward him. "How long have you known this one?" He glanced at Sharkey, then his gaze darted down to Xander's collar.

"She greeted me when we docked." Simon got an 'ahha' look on his face, so Xander casually scratched his neck and activated his collar so he could quickly explained his concerns about her allegiance.

Simon sat down and groomed one ear for a moment, as he clandestinely sent an 'understood' message back to Xander. Rising to his paws, Simon said, "Tango, my friend, do you think you could do another casual fly-over of the place?"

"Si, me Maestro." With that, he opened his wings, made a couple running jump-steps and took to the air.

Sharkey stared after the bird in obvious confusion, then turned to Xander. "What was that all about?"

"I think its called aerial reconnaissance."

"Exactly," Simon said.

"Of what?"

"What do you think?" Xander asked.

"I imagine it involves why you came here, but I still haven't figured that one out."

"Why did you come with me?"

"Meeting you was the greatest thing that has ever happened to me and I didn't have anything I wanted to do more." She glanced at Simon, then quickly looked down. Her nose turned deep red and she began muttering to her paws. "Until I met you, that is."

Simon scratched his neck and batted an ear. "Why do you say that? I'm nothing special, just a translator for kitten tales."

"But everyone knows who you are." She risked a quick look at Xander. "Everyone knows who both of you are."

"You don't own any humans, do you?" Simon asked. She shook her head. "Well, once we're finished touring this area, perhaps we can change that."

She sat bolt upright. "And become slaves like you?" She violently shook her head. "No thank you." Simon's ears raised. "Well look at you, both of you are wearing collars, for Hathor's sake! Do you really think I'm eager to have some two-foot strap one of those things around my neck? I see how badly they bother you and how you keep scratching at them."

"Have you ever had a collar?" Xander asked.

"For a couple days when I was very young, but I got rid of it as soon as possible." She raised her chin. Though her nose was still bright red, her eyes were flashing with anger.

Xander and Simon exchanged a look, each wondering if she was trying to get information about the technology built into their collars or if she actually was that ignorant. Regardless, until they were sure of her loyalty, it was best not to reveal too much. Besides, even though Peppy was being quiet as a shadow, he was still there and even though Simon was certain that the mongoose was an ally, it was best not to publicize Catamondo's secrets. Xander stopped scratching and sighed, "Is there somewhere we can go that doesn't have so many biting bugs?"

"Sure," Simon said. "Up ahead there is a great view of the river." He turned to go.

"Why do you guys have such an obsession with water?" Sharkey demanded. "Its unnatural, you know."

"Why do you say that?" Simon asked.

"Well, he," Sharkey flicked an ear at Xander, "lives on a boat and has been swimming twice. Now, you want to look at water."

"It's quite lovely from a distance," Simon said.

"Does that mean you don't plan to swim?" she asked.

"Only when necessary."

"Are you saying that you have done it? Or that you know how to swim? Or what?"

Simon batted at a bug near his ear and shrugged. "You used to live on a boat. Are you telling me you never fell in?"

"How do you know that?"

Simon tilted his head toward Xander. "He told me."

"And just how did he do that?"

"I emailed him before we left," Xander said.

Sharkey's eyes narrowed. "That is true." Xander heard a 'but' coming and knew she was about to confront him with the fact that she had told him about living aboard a Grand

Banks after washing off the rotten fish, so he pointed both ears at Peppy and gave her 'the look'. Sharkey clamped her jaws shut, and swished her tail with annoyance.

Chapter 9

Simon and Xander studied the high walls surrounding the sun-drenched compound and the low buildings inside.

"Looks like a private park," Sharkey said.

"Looks like a canine training center to me," Xander said.

"Looks like easy fishing in the pond," Peppy said.

"Looks like Dame Esmeralda can freely move around the compound," Simon said.

"You've met her and can identify her from this distance?" Xander asked. Simon nodded. "Does she seem the same?"

"She isn't wearing her pearls."

"You can tell from this distance?" Xander wasn't even close enough to be positive of her markings, so either Simon had amazing eyesight or he knew Dame Esmeralda extremely well, or he was merely claiming that the light-colored Norwegian Forest Cat was Dame Esmeralda. And if that was the case, why?

"She's a friend of the family."

"What exactly do you mean by that?" Sharkey demanded. Xander wanted to know the answer to that, too, and suspected it might explain why Simon notified

Lady Montgomery directly, instead of putting the information through the normal channels.

Simon wrapped his fluffy tail around his toes, like a shield, then muttered, "She's my godmother."

Xander blinked.

Sharkey's mouth dropped open.

Peppy asked, "Is it my imagination or does it look like the dogs are obeying her?"

All three cats turned their attention back to the distant compound, where Dame Esmeralda did seem to be overseeing the training of the dogs. Xander scratched his ear, and cued his collar's volume receptor, though the voice was faint, he could distinguish the words, "Purrrfect Popo. I am very proud of you." She seemed to be speaking to a brown puppy, who was rolling in the grass with excitement. When it was finished rolling, it hopped up, crawled to her and appeared to kiss her toes.

Xander clicked off the feature, stared at Simon and asked, "Exactly how long she has been affiliating with dogs?"

"Aside from Duke and Duchess?" Simon shrugged.

"And they are?"

"Members of her family." Xander stared at Simon, wondering how much other crucial information he had withheld. "Explain exactly why you contacted -"

Simon quickly said, "Fine, but not here or now."

"Why not?" Simon glared at him. Xander's claws itched to smack the smug kid. "Because of you, I have spent days trying to sort this mess out instead of finish the emergency-preparedness project I was working on."

Xander looked at Sharkey and Peppy, "I'm sure all of us, including your bird-friend had other things they could be doing, instead of go chasing around these mountains and getting eaten by bugs." Or landing in rotten fish, which he could still smell between his toes, no matter how many times he'd washed them.

"It was my only option."

"Somehow, I doubt that."

"No one would listen to me."

Xander studied the boy through squinted eyes. "You never brought the problem to my attention before it became a crisis. Exactly what are we dealing with?" He leaned so close that their noses nearly touched and lowered his voice, "I want the truth and if I even get a whiff of a red herring, you will regret it to your dying day."

Simon stood up on trembling paws. "Fine, but not here." He took an unsteady step deeper into the underbrush. "Peppy, keep an eye on the compound and see if you can find any weak spots in their defenses."

Xander looked at Sharkey. "I would appreciate it if you helped him."

Though her ears were nearly flat against her head, she nodded.

Once they were deep in the foliage, Xander spun to face Simon. "Talk and do not leave anything out!"

Simon swallowed. "How well do you know her?"

"Who? Sharkey? Esmeralda?"

"Both, actually."

"I met Sharkey when we docked in this country and only

know Esmeralda by pedigree. What difference does that make?"

"I'm not sure, but you might have noticed that this island has an extremely large dog population." Xander nodded as he swished his whiskers to urge Simon to continue. "Training centers are not the only thing we have a lot of. I can't prove it, but I believe there are also laboratories which conduct psychological projects."

"Are you suggesting that either Sharkey or Esmeralda might have been brainwashed or something?

"It's possible."

"Then why not me?"

"No time."

"Well, based on that factor, how am I supposed to know that you haven't had your thoughts twisted?"

Simon's eyes widened. "We can't know, can we?"

Xander studied the boy's expression and decided it would be best to calm him. "Have any of your collar's alerts been triggered?" Simon shook his head. "Then it is unlikely that your thoughts have been compromised." Xander narrowed his eyes as he studied him. "You are aware that the gems are programmed to be compatible with our individual thought patterns, correct?"

"I did hear something about that."

"Well, then, if your collar is fine, you probably are, too."

Simon licked his upper lip. "So, what does that say about Sharkey and Esmeralda?" Xander perked his ears, urging him to be specific. "Your little friend doesn't have a collar and Esmeralda's got broken a couple months ago. At least that's what she said, but I would have thought she would have had it repaired by now."

"Big problem, isn't it?"

"Are you beginning to understand why I went into a panic and contacted Lady Montgomery as soon as I realized her sister had disappeared?"

"I think so. However, to deal with this mess, I need facts, so can you please begin with the first time you thought or felt there could be a problem with Esmeralda?"

"Well, that would be the first time I actually saw her – when I was two weeks old and my eyes were finally open – and realized that Duke, who everyone knew was her dear friend, was a poodle."

If Xander hadn't already been sitting down, he would have landed, hard, on his tail. He took a deep breath, held it for the count of ten, then blew it out. "Dear friend."

Simon nodded. "It was a big surprise."

"May I ask if your parents knew about Duke when they named Esmeralda your godmother?"

Simon nodded. "I think it was mainly a political move, but they really like her, and I don't think they would have done it purely for politics."

Xander silently studied Simon, before he said, "Makes sense. Lady Montgomery would already have been well-known when you were born." He scratched a bug bite on his ear. "I take it that her only oddity is having a canine for a friend?"

"As far as I know." Simon wrapped his tail around his toes, in a defensive posture. "Actually, he is a good guy and aside from his looks, he thinks and acts a lot like a cat."

Years of gathering information enabled Xander to appear calm. "She's not the first cat to have a dog for a friend. I, myself, know a couple honorable canines." Simon visibly relaxed. "Much as we would like to believe otherwise, we cats are not the only intelligent species." A pretty yellow butterfly fluttered by. "Sometimes, I wonder how many species believe that they are the superior one."

"Humans sure think so."

Xander nodded in agreement. "Perhaps, one of these centuries, our scientists will figure out a way we can control them better and stop them from killing each other over silly things."

"They do seem to have an inordinate interest in power and profit."

"But with a pitiful understanding of what is actually valuable. However, that is not a problem that you and I need to deal with, today. And I need to know the actual situation, not something designed to get help, so please begin from the moment you realized something was wrong and you needed help and do not stop talking until you fully explain all you know about this country's dog situation and how it relates to the facility Esmeralda is at."

Simon started talking and didn't stop for over two hours.

Chapter 10

The setting rays of the sun painted the stark-white, concrete walls of the compound in shades of orange, red and burnt umber. "Red sky at night, sailor's delight. Red sky in the morning, sailors take warning," Xander muttered. He hoped this was a promising sign and tried not to think about how closely the darker tones resembled the color of blood.

"What?" Sharkey asked.

Had she heard that? "Nothing, its just a saying I was thinking about."

"A saying. About sailors." She looked heavenward. "And you say my quotes are weird."

"And you think quoting Indian tribes is more sensible?"

"I don't just quote native tribes." He raised a brow. She looked down at her toes. "Our life is what our thoughts make it. Marcus Aurelius said that and I think it says a lot and he wasn't an Indian."

"Well, who was he?"

"I don't know, but he wasn't an Indian."

Xander assured himself that the sky was red, and things should be fine, then he sighed. "Nothing ventured;

nothing gained." He got up and took a step toward the path, which led to the compound's gate. The thing that bothered him more than anything else was the fact that the gate was ajar, because he had a horrible feeling that the dogs expected him and the slightly open gate was the gaping jaws of a trap.

Sharkey scrambled to her feet and came after him. "I'm coming, too."

"Great."

"Don't sound so happy."

"Why should I be happy?"

"I am helping."

"If you say so."

"What is wrong with you? Ever since your friend Simon arrived, you've been snappy as a squirrel."

Xander stomped down the path for several minutes without saying a word. He had to get his emotions under control and the best way to do that was clear the air. "How come you hate collars?" he asked in what he hoped was a casual tone.

"Why do you think that?"

"You don't wear one."

"Just because I've only ever had an itchy flea collar, doesn't mean I hate them, but I certainly don't see any reason for wearing an emblem of slavery, so yeah, maybe I do hate them. You were smart to notice that."

"What do you mean your collar was itchy?"

She snorted. "It gave me a rash, so I got rid of it. Where do you get the ridiculous idea that this is important?"

He stopped and turned to face her. "You were issued a flea collar?"

"That's what I said." She stared at him. "Again, why is this so important to you?"

"I've never met anyone who hadn't owned a real collar." He scratched his own.

"Well, now you have. Look, in case you haven't already figured it out, I don't have a pedigree and I'm not some hoity-toity cat, with owners who buy them fancy baubles." Tears welled in his eyes. "I'd hoped that you liked me for just being me, but I guess that was stupid, because you only like girls with pedigrees and pink collars with glitzy diamond studs."

'Pink collars with glitzy diamond studs' "Are you talking about Fluffy?" As she nodded, a tear fell. "What does she have to do with this?"

"Everything." Sharkey sniffed.

Xander blinked in confusion. Why did Fluffy's collar of office bother her, when his own sapphires and Simon's tiger eyes didn't seem to? "Are you jealous?" She hung her head, refusing to answer the question, and that was answer enough. "Fluffy is my friend, not my girlfriend."

"So you didn't give her the collar?"

He blinked at the startling question. "Of course not... how could you... why would you..." He paused and frowned, as he thought over what she had told him. "Didn't your parents register your birth?"

"How would I know? I don't even know their names. All I know is that when I was two days old, my mother was run over while crossing the road and some humans took me in and fed me with bottles from a doll." Her nose turned red. "When the kittens living on the dock found out about that, they laughed at me, then shunned me."

"What do you know about Catamondo?" He sat down and stared at her, knowing that they needed to resolve this before walking into some trap.

"Cat a what?"

"Many millennia ago, Hathor organized our species, and yes, there do seem to be an exceptionally high number of pedigrees in the highest offices, but each and every cat that has been born is part of it and once every kitten is six months old, they are given a flea collar, as their graduation gift from basic education."

"Well, this is the first I've ever heard about anything fancy like that."

He studied her. "But you knew who I was and who Simon were."

"Well, duh! I can read the Daily Mews."

Xander rose and with a swish of his tail, started toward the compound's gate. "Right now, I need to find out what is going on with Esmeralda, but just as soon as I get that sorted, I'll take care of your problems."

"Don't bother. I've always gotten along just fine. You don't need to waste your precious time on me."

"Hush."

"Why? So you can continue to tell me I'm a problem? Well, I am not, and I'm certainly not yours."

"Fine. But for now, please be quiet. That gate should be locked and since it isn't, it could be a trap, so could you please be quiet so I can listen for clues?"

She clamped her jaws together and nodded.

He stayed where he was until the sun settled beyond the distant trees. Though there was still enough light to see, there were also many lovely shadows to melt into, which was perfect for infiltrating the compound, or for foiling a plot, if his straight-forward approach did not work. Nighttime noises seemed normal, so he moved to the center of the path and strolled toward the gate, as if he was an invited guest.

Xander walked through the gate alert for an ambush, a watcher, or anything hostile, though he tried to appear oblivious. His collar gave a faint vibration, which meant that he had stepped through a laser beam, so someone knew he had arrived. He stepped to the side of the path and glanced back at Sharkey, who seemed to be attempting to copy his relaxed attitude.

The gravel path wound through a well-tended garden. Off to the right, there were two buildings, which he suspected were barracks, but the main path curved to the left down the hill. Despite the fact that the laser should have alerted them to his arrival, all stayed quiet. They were certainly cool customers and that generally meant professionals.

He waited a few long minutes, still close enough to the gate for a hasty escape, but the only thing that happened was that night fully set in and distant bats squeaked as they left their lair to forage.

Sharkey chewed her lower lip, but didn't make a sound.

Xander nodded, and began to walk down the winding path toward the main building. Sharkey kept pace behind him, close enough to watch his back – or stab it, if that was her intent – but not close enough to get in his way and accidentally be injured by an erroneously placed kick, if they were attacked.

They passed a water fountain, the waterlily covered fish pond that Peppy had admired and 2 greenhouses; the large one on the left was filled with vegetables and spices, Though he was tempted, he did not pause to inspect the catnip. The smaller greenhouse seemed to be devoted to flowers, probably orchids, though he didn't know much about plants.

At the bottom of he hill, a meter-wide shallow stream covered the path and a plank was conveniently laid across it. Instead of potentially stepping on the trigger for a trap, Xander jumped onto the rich, dark dirt of a garden on the other side, and sank up to his knees in slick, stagnant muck.

A giggle, from behind him was quickly muffled. He looked over his shoulder. Sharkey was standing on the plank, lips clamped together and eyes crinkled with mirth.

It was a struggle to extract each paw and step backward into the flowing stream, but he eventually managed to get all four legs deep enough in the running water to start washing away the reeking slime.

"Three is a charm," Sharkey whispered.

He ignored her.

"Guests should stay on the path," a refined, but slightly accented voice said.

Xander turned his attention toward the speaker. "Good advice, but a bit too late."

"True," the unseen speaker said. "Once you get the worst off, it would be wise to wash with lemon juice because muck from the bog garden has a lot of fish-waste in it and if you wash with lemon, it cuts the smell."

"Again, good advice. Thanks."

Sharkey walked toward the darkest shadow and bashfully introduced herself.

"A pleasure to meet you. I am Duchess." Xander's fur stood on end, as he finally recognized the slightly odd accent – dog. He shot out of the water, as if propelled by a rocket and landed next to Sharkey.

"Wow!" Duchess said, "No wonder Ms. Mitzi calls you the Kamikaze. Very impressive, but you really should clean with lemon juice."

"She's right," another unknown voice said. "As soon as you have, we can all have a nice chat." He stared at the source of the voice, but could only make out a medium-large, light-colored shape, that seemed to be the correct dimensions for Dame Esmeralda.

"Dame Esmeralda, I presume?"

The form stepped forward and, indeed, was an elegant long-haired white cat, which looked a lot like his pal, Merlin. Since Merlin was related to Lady Montgomery, and thereby Dame Esmeralda, it was logical for them to look similar in the shadows.

Suddenly, flood lights lit the area, blinding him. He tensed for an attack, but nothing happened. Eyes watering, both from the glare and the stink of rotten fish-waste, Xander fought to regain his grasp of the situation.

"Sorry about that," another unknown voice said, "but I have never been able to see as well in the dark as you, and my old eyes are not improving with age." The voice had a dog accent and seemed quite old. When Xander finally managed to get an eye open, he saw a large black poodle, with a graying muzzle and rich, red ascot sitting on the right side of an elegant white Norwegian Forest Cat, who could have been Lady Montgomery's double and on her left was a much younger black female poodle wearing a glittery pink bow. Obviously, the dogs were Duke and Duchess.

Xander blinked, but the image didn't go away, it simply became sharper. "So, you weren't catnapped."

Leaf-green eyes widened for a brief moment, before Esmeralda tipped her head back and laughed, while the dogs howled with mirth.

Sharkey looked at him, but Xander was not certain exactly why they found his statement so funny, so he shrugged. Finally, after several minutes, Esmeralda, managed to ask, "Was that what Moomoo told you to motivate you to leave the Bahamian survey?"

Moomoo? "If you are referring to Lady Montgomery, then yes, that is what I was told, but I believe she got the information from Sir Simon."

Duchess woofed out a big laugh, "I told you he had more of a talent for fiction than you gave him credit for."

Disoriented, and not feeling as if he was in danger, Xander was tempted to sit down, but if he did that, the nasty slime could spread to uncontaminated fur, so he stood and tried to analyze how a red claw situation could have been called based on an exaggeration. The rating system needed a better check and balance, at the very least.

"So, you know about the Bahamian survey?"

"Well. of course I do. dear bov." Esmeralda said. "since I

was the one who told Moomoo that we really needed the islands surveyed and safety bunkers built in areas that are prone to hurricanes."

"Oh."

"True," Duke said. "After so many died during the last hurricane, we realized it was an issue. Valentine is doing something similar for the dogs, but is having quite a problem controlling his human." The three of them chuckled. Xander tried to get his thoughts to accept that Valentine's rank among the dogs must be similar to his own.

"His human is helping," Duchess said, "just not in the way that Valentine wants."

"He should have expected that," Esmeralda said, "after all, his human is a veterinarian. It should have been expected that he would see the plight of the island dogs and wish to help." She glanced at Duke. "He just never imagined that his human's way of helping would be to set up clinics everywhere. Or think that spaying and neutering was the best way to deal with things."

"He is correct about it being effective to control the STDs and make sure the population doesn't expand too much for the available resources," Duke pointed out.

"That's why they always set up the big tent on the beach?" Xander asked. The other three nodded.

"You're talking about the slobbery red dog, right?" Sharkey asked. Xander nodded. "That explains a lot."

"Meaning?"

"Well, half the dogs who welcomed him were happy to see him, but the rest were calling his boat the butcher ship and other not very flattering things."

How had he missed that? "Dialect?" She nodded.

"Well, let us not just stand here. Xander, my boy, you need to get those paws cleaned before the muck dries and makes it ten times harder. Duchess, why don't you take Miss Sharkey into the dojo for a snack?" She turned to Duke, "Could you assist Xander while I send a very succinct note to my idiot godson and tell him to get down here, instead of hide."

"That mongoose is with him," Duchess said, "What if he brings it?"

'Then we finally meet the rascal."

"You know where he is?" The words burst from Xander before he could control them.

"Well of course, dear boy. Why else would we leave the gate open in invitation?"

Why else, indeed? "How?"

Duchess snickered as she said, "I've known Simple Simon my whole life. Don't you think I know his pals? And don't you think that twit Tango stuck out like a sore paw when he kept flying overhead?"

"We watched where he landed," Duke said with a shrug.

Chapter 11

Clean, damp legs smelling of lemons, Xander entered the dojo, a roofed area with training mats covering the floor. One side of the area was a concrete wall of what he suspected was the main house. The white stucco beneath was barely visible behind the impressive display of antique and modern combat weapons. Xander had been in many feline dojos, but never in a private one with such opulence. Hearing footsteps, he tore his attention away from the collection and turned to the door. Recognizing Simon's tread, he sat on the dojo's semi-soft workout mat in time to watch how Dame Esmeralda interacted with Sir Simon.

"So, instead of emailing or messaging me or any one of other means you had available to directly contact me, you decided the wisest move was to twist a few facts and involve Moomoo," Dame Esmeralda snapped, the moment Simon's paw passed the threshold. "Does that about cover it?"

Though Simon appeared strong and fit, he also appeared to look for a hole to disappear into, as he slithered the rest of the way into the room. "I did try to contact you, but you had disappeared."

"From the Kingston house?" Simon nodded. Esmeralda looked heavenward, as she asked. "Did it ever occur to you that our Kingston house is the property of the British Consulate?" Simon blinked in confusion. Dame Esmeralda looked at him as if his IQ was lower than a bedbug's. "Well, it is. And since your human is the Canadian Ambassador, whose accommodation is actually owned by the Canadian Government, your situation would be the same as ours, if your human passed away."

"You had to leave because Sir Cochran died?"

"Well, duh!" Duchess said.

"Why didn't any of you say something?" Simon looked around for support, for a moment, his attention fastened outside, where statues of Bastet, a cat god, and Anubis, the dog's main god, stood side by side, overlooking the gardens and dojo.

"Dear, dear boy," Duke said, "in the eulogy at his memorial service, I said that we were lucky to have such a good human that he made certain of our needs, even after death by willing us this five acre parcel and enough funds to cover our needs for several years. Weren't you listening?"

Xander sighed. "I am sorry for your loss. Your human sounds like he was exceptional. However, the how and why you moved from Kingston doesn't interest me as much as why you have an amazing dojo like this and why I saw so many puppies being trained here."

"Simple-" Duchess said.

"This is a fulfillment of a lifetime dream," Esmeralda and Duke said in unison. Duke motioned for her to continue. "When I initially adopted Sir Robert Cochran, I didn't realize he already belonged to Duke." She gave her friend an apologetic look. "So, when I initially moved in, there was a great deal of tension."

Duke barked out a harsh laugh. "That's her polite way of telling you I tried to murder her. Don't look so shocked, it's the truth. Fortunately, she wasn't particularly easy to kill."

"Why fortunately?" Xander asked.

"Because if I had been successful killing her, she wouldn't have been alive to save my life."

Xander clamped his jaws together for fear of saying the wrong thing, and thus not hearing the complete explanation.

"As usual, Duke is exaggerating," Esmeralda said. "All I did was tell him some information. Actually, I only repeated a weather report."

"About a hurricane," Duke said, "which was something I didn't understand, since we had only recently arrived here and it was the first hurricane I had encountered." Duke bowed his head to Esmeralda. "The dogs on this island have a very primitive communication system."

"The midnight howl," Simon said.

Duke nodded. "But though there are not as many cats, most, if not all, seem to have access to global information." Sharkey's eyes widened and she gave Xander a quick glance. He inclined his head in answer to her unspoken question. "If Esmeralda had not warned me to get our human to change plans, we would have died, as so many others did."

"The amazing thing is that he actually listened to me, then when he realized I wasn't just some dumb ball of fur, he began to treat me like an individual." Esmeralda smiled fondly at Duke. "And from there, we have grown to become best friends and allies... It wasn't his fault for thinking as he originally did. He was raised to believe dogs were superior. I was raised to believe dogs were demons. But we had just arrived in Jamaica, so my support system was an ocean away, all I had was Duke and Robert. If they had died in the storm, I would have had serious problems, so it was quite self-serving to explain the approaching weather system to him."

Duchess nodded. "If you let them, they'll give you a blow by blow account of the storm and its aftermath. The cliff-notes version is that they learned they would have a better life getting along together than living a cold war, and once they threw away their prejudices, and got to really know each other, they decided that the world would be a much better place if we all focused on what makes each of us good, instead of our differences." She looked at Simon. "Simple has figured out a lot of this." Simon stared at her in surprise. "Hello! Earth to Simple Simon, what are Tango and Peppy?" He looked at her in confusion. "Granted, they aren't dogs, but they aren't cats, either."

"So?"

"So you, above most cats, should realize that species does not matter. Character matters. Deeds matter."

"Good intentions-"

"Do not matter, particularly when the results are bad. And most importantly, words do not matter." Duchess glared at him. "With the possible exception of lies. And Simple, you lied for no good reason."

"I had a perfectly good reason."

"What was it?"

"Esmeralda had disappeared with a bunch of dogs."

"A bunch of dogs! We are her family! How would you like it if someone said that you had disappeared with a psycho bird and a bandit?"

Simon snorted. "Don't lower yourself to insulting Tango and Peppy just to try and make a point."

Duchess's chocolate eyes gleamed as she leaned close and said, "I was quoting from a message you wrote. Jorge forwarded it to Aunt Esmeralda." Simon gasped. Duchess woofed. "How does it feel when someone gossips and slanders like you did, then gets caught?"

Simon's attention dropped to his toes.

Duke cleared his throat. "I believe that has sorted out a great deal of the problem."

Xander inclined his head. "Indeed. This situation brings to mind something my friend, Holly, said, 'Words are wind. Unless they're backed up by actions that match them, they are meaningless.' When Holly said that, she was telling me how she gauged an individual's true character, and it seems to me this can easily cross species lines."

"I totally agree," Esmeralda said. "And that is why we all felt it was so important to teach the young to see the individual instead of the species."

"Sir Cochran said humans waged war about pigeon holes," Duchess added. "We never want our species to degenerate to that level."

"Why would humans fight bird holes?" Sharkey asked.

"Pigeon holes are what Sir Cochran called the way humans labeled things. For instance, he loved to harp about how humans murdered millions just because one group called their god by one name and another group called the same entity by another name."

Duke woofed. "Dear man would get quite worked up over the millions who had been killed in the name of a god who instructed man not to kill."

"So you are training puppies because of the way humans fight over religion," Sharkey said.

"That is only one silly thing that they kill over. It seems humans war over color, nationality, resources, national borders, politics … just about anything where they can find a difference."

"Your views seem remarkably similar to the values I was raised with," Xander said. "Do most dogs share this opinion?"

"Hardly!" Duke woofed. "Which is why it is so important to teach the young to see the world as it is and to think for themselves, instead of blindly follow propaganda."

Though he wasn't particularly comfortable agreeing with a canine, the dog was right. Xander nodded in agreement. "I have met a few honorable dogs that would probably agree with you, but most seem to be intent upon world domination."

Duchess laughed, "Most dogs would say the same thing about cats."

"Agreed," Xander said. "Do you think one small training center can have a major impact on world view?"

"An acorn, given the proper place and nutrients can grow into a mighty oak," Esmeralda's emerald eyes sparkled. "Of course, this takes time and patience... I will probably only see a tiny sprout in my lifetime, but at least, when I die, I will know that I planted the seed."

Chapter 12

As the first rays of dawn warmed the eastern sky, the soft, muted sounds of night were shattered by a chorus of crowing roosters. Xander's ears flattened against his head, but that did little to soften the horrible noise.

Duke, who had been explaining the intricacies of the training program sighed, then suggested they go inside for breakfast.

Old-timey clocks were correct twice a day and sometimes even dogs came up with excellent ideas. Xander stood up and stretched. As he rose, he heard other activity from the two houses up the hill and knew the puppies were getting up. It would be interesting to find out how they reacted when they actually met and, unless they were all good actors, it could tell him if Esmeralda's training was actually giving the puppies objectivity.

Too many times, it was easy to see what one wanted to see instead of what actually was. Xander flicked his tail. If educating puppies actually worked, longterm, it would be wise to learn as much as possible about Esmeralda's project, but, in truth, for the long haul, he preferred Valentine's human's approach. Despite the fact that neutering improved the longevity of the dogs and their general health, it also cleaned riffraff out of the gene-pool. And any way he looked at it, eliminating future generations of dogs was a wonderful idea. He wondered why Catamondo's governing boards had never thought about sponsoring free neutering clinics for dogs.

When he got back to Whispurring Winds, he would conduct a study of C Pause's operation, write it up and send in the report. Even if he had to spend time with Valentine. He shivered, but remained resolute.

After an excellent breakfast of chicken pot pie, Xander quietly approached the soft sounds of movement in the dojo. From his angle, he could see Duchess, who seemed to be doing a somewhat stiff version of tàijíquán, which felines had been teaching to kittens for over five-thousand years. Duchess, who was younger than he was, was not as limber as he was, which was good to know. Chin up and tail high, he wondered if her abilities were typical; then, he wondered why he had never thought about the flexibility of dogs' anatomy previously.

On whisper-soft paws, he moved into a deep shadow, which allowed him to observe the training session, while his back was protected from a sneak attack. It was the ideal spot to observe the dojo from, without bringing attention to himself or making it look like he was hiding, which would have been a politically bad move.

To his surprise, Sharkey had joined the thirteen puppies Duchess was training and though Sharkey was more limber, she tripped over her own paws more frequently, as the flow changed from one movement to the next.

What was the world coming to when fourteen dogs could appear more coordinated than a cat?

When the session ended, the military-precise ranks broke up and most of the puppies crowded around Sharkey, as if she was visiting royalty. In his five years of life, Xander had never seen anything so strange.

"Well, what do you think?" Duchess asked.

Xander controlled his startled reaction. "Interesting." He admitted, embarrassed at being so focused on the puppies and Sharkey that a dog had managed to sneak up on him. "How long have you been training this group?"

"Most of them, just a week, but Mouse – the one with the big ears and grayish fur – has been doing this for three years."

His ears perked as he studied the smallest puppy, who was less than half his size. "Years?" The little guy didn't look over three month's old.

Duchess nodded. "In many ways, this training program began because of him."

"How so?"

"Well, as you can see, he's small." Duchess cleared her throat. "He has been from birth and years ago, Dad and Aunt Essy felt sorry for him and wanted to do something."

"Sharkey seems to be making friends."

"Aside from Aunt Essy, she's probably the only other cat they've ever seen." Seeing his expression, she added, "I'm serious. In case you haven't noticed, there are quite a few dogs in Jamaica, but not too many cats."

"I had noticed." He frowned. "May I ask a question?" She inclined her head. "Ever since I arrived in the islands, I've been seeing medium sized, short-haired brown dogs."

"Island dogs."

"Ah, I'd never heard of the breed, but they seem quite widespread."

"They aren't what you call a breed. They are the product of the natural course of selection."

He blinked as he looked at the brown puppies. "They are all similar in size and musculature. Are you sure they aren't members of an unofficial breed?"

"Positive." And she sounded certain. "Those traits are what occur anywhere our species develops in isolation. That said, I admit there is debate about whether what you are looking at is a process of natural selection or if, after a few generations, the genes return to the basics."

"Fascinating." What was equally fascinating what that he was sitting in the shade of a sweet-scented tree and having an intelligent discussion with a dog. "Let me guess, the shade of brown is an ideal camouflage and the size is optimal for whatever food is available."

"Precisely." Duchess looked at him with appreciation. "Would you like to meet them?"

No, but he could not say that. Instead, Xander stood up and motioned for Duchess to lead the way. He wasn't certain what he'd expected, but the thirteen puppies treated him the same way kittens did – with adoration. It was difficult to remain objective when every canine in sight seemed to think he was a feline god.

Before Xander figured out how he had been talked into it, he and Mouse were in the center of the dojo and everyone, including Dame Esmeralda, Simon, and Duke were seated on the thin strip of lawn between the dojo and the pond over which Bastet and Anubis's statues presided. He knew how he had gotten talked into the impending kickboxing exhibition, and wondered if Mouse, who was half his size, had volunteered because of his size or because he was considered the one with the most training or simply because his big ears and kinky, grayish fur looked foolish compared to the sleek brown fur of the other students.

Duchess held everyone's attention as she announced the rules they were to follow – rules that were identical to a Catamondo kickboxing tournament. Xander glanced at Esmeralda and raised a brow. She smiled and gave a slight nod, as she admitted the information had come from her. A slight movement on the other side of the pond caught Xander's attention and a glint of brown eye made him suspect that Peppy had come to observe the impromptu exhibition. Though tempted to look upward for Tango, Xander forced himself to keep his attention on Mouse's eyes and Duchess's voice.

With a deep, vibrating sound, one of the puppies hit the ancient cymbal and the first round began. As the reverberation bent the air, Xander's spine arched and his ears flattened against his head. He moved with lighting-fast speed and lashed at Mouse's head, but missed. Surprised by the puppy's ability to avoid the blow, he completed a twisting turn and landed on his toes, just in time to bend backward and avoid Mouse's lunge.

Either the boy was better trained than he'd expected or he'd been lucky two moves in a row. And Xander didn't believe in luck. But he did believe in practice and training. Now that he no longer expected an immediate win, he watched Mouse's moves and gained appreciation for the little guy's skill. While he wasn't as flexible as a cat and totally capable of precise execution of some of the moves, he made up for his lack with the strength, cunning and stamina of his attacks.

Though the kid was good, Xander was able to hold back

his best moves, which made for a relatively even match. The puppies woofed and yipped with excitement, their support equally given to whomever made an excellent move and their jeers to whoever blundered.

They were the most bizarre audience Xander had ever had.

Xander divided his attention between Mouse and covert glances at the audience and determined that at least one of the puppies might be moles sent from a more typical dog training facility.

Twice, Peppy got so enthralled in the match than he inched forward, so that by the end of round two, he had moved out of the shadows far enough for his nose to be visible.

As the gong reverberated the end of the third round, Xander and Mouse bowed to each other, then turned to bow to the audience, who was already rushing toward them.

A melee of congratulations erupted, though Xander had made sure there was no obvious winner, just as he had made sure no blood was drawn. He inclined his head, accepting whatever approval was given to him, and privately agreed that he had done an amazing job of holding back not only his skills, but his inclination to shred noses.

"How do you do that?" Sharkey asked.

"Do what, exactly?" Xander asked.

"Go from relaxed to full-fledged attack, then from full battle mode to bow?" She batted an ear in confusion.

"Practice. Years and years of practice."

"That's what I figured you were going to say." She looked glum. "I'm way far behind everyone else my age, aren't I?"

"Well, you're certainly on a different path, but who is to say that it is behind the others?" Esmeralda said. "The question you must ask yourself is if you are comfortable with the path you're on."

Sharkey violently shook her head. "I've felt lost for most of my life."

"Do you still feel that way?" Esmeralda's tone was kind.

"Not quite so much since meeting him and Simon." Sharkey glanced at him, then quickly turned her attention to her paws, her nose a flaming red.

"Then it might be a time for a new direction." Esmeralda smiled. "You are the only one who can feel what is right for you, but you seem to get along well with the other students and I would like you to consider joining us here, at least for this term."

"Are you serious?" Sharkey exclaimed.

Was she, Xander wondered. Esmeralda inclined her head. "It would be nice to have another girl, not to mention cat around here and our goal has always been to have the school integrated. You do not need to decide right now, but I hope you think about it."

Xander edged away from the center of the group, scratched his collar and accessed Whispurring Winds' security system. All was well and his programs were working so well that his humans still had not realized he was away on a mission. Though none of his covert cameras were in an ideal position to check the activity at the dogs' training facility in the mangroves, he was able to verify that C Pause's decks were clear of trash bags and their strange tent was set up on the beach, where there seemed to be a lot of activity. He would check this out in detail upon his return.

Over a lovely trout lunch, the conversation veered to the fact that humans in powerful positions tended to own dogs, not cats. Esmeralda, who was seated next to him, leaned close and softly said, "I always wanted to research and determine if people in power need blind subservience or if they are so power-hungry no cat will adopt them." She batted an ear. "I began researching the US presidents. Did you know that Abraham Lincoln is purported to be the first president to be owned by a cat?"

"No, I hadn't heard that," Xander admitted. History was not a topic he focused on.

"He was a good man, who was owned by Tabby and Dixie. In fact, Lincoln once remarked that Dixie was 'smarter than my whole cabinet', so the man was obviously was quite smart and well trained. Unfortunately, after he was assassinated, it took years for Catamondo to regain control. McKinley was owned by a pair of Angora kittens, but the records don't show anything noteworthy. Slippers and Tom Quartz owned Theodore Roosevelt, but that man was nearly impossible to direct, and continually pestered them by bringing all manner of creatures into the family." Dame Esmeralda's eyes flashed with emotion. "Would you believe that the fool man brought home everything from poultry to snakes and rodents? I think the worst was the badger. I have never heard of a badger having a good disposition, so the dreadful creature must have made things quite distracting. It's no wonder that Slippers and Tom Quartz had such difficulty training him."

Xander coughed. Apparently Dame Esmeralda wasn't as blind to the differences between the species as he had begun to fear. And he had never met anyone with such a good grasp of American history, particularly a British dame. All he knew for a fact was that American politicians were much more prone to being owned by dogs, and several seemed to be owned by a pack. Now that he thought about it, he realized how alarming that was. "Dogs do seem blind to the characters of their humans, don't they?"

She inclined her head in agreement. "They also tend to view themselves as the pet, instead of the correct way." She glanced around to see if anyone else might be listening. Satisfied that her comments were private, she went on, "Duke and Duchess even acted that way with Sir Cochran, but it worked for them and him, as well. The differences between our species and the way we handle things are very interesting, but I still prefer to focus on the areas we are the same."

A rousing round of woofs peppered with a rew-reow came from the far corner of the eating area, where Sharkey and Mouse were sharing a water bowl. "They seem to be getting along well," Xander said.

"Indeed," Esmeralda agreed. "How do you feel about that?"

"I beg your pardon?"

"You heard my question. She is your friend. What are you feeling right now?"

"She's a good kid, but not exactly a close friend." He shrugged.

"So you would have no objection to her staying here?"

"That is her choice, not mine. Just as it was her choice to come here."

"She and Mouse seem to like each other." He batted an ear in agreement.

"Have you contacted Moomoo and explained things?"

"I left Lady Montgomery a message, but don't know when she will check her machine." Xander frowned. "She put a red claw on my orders, so I don't understand why she wouldn't give communications from you priority."

Dame Esmeralda shrugged. "Sometimes cat behavior can be as baffling as a dog's."

How true.

Chapter 13

Xander, Simon and Sharkey spent a week at Esmeralda's training camp. During the visit, Simon spent most of his time outside the compound with Tango and Peppy.

Sharkey spent most of her time with Mouse and it was apparent that they had become close friends. Xander theorized that a large portion of their attraction might be due to sharing a similar background. He realized his wasn't the only one with that opinion when Duchess commented that Mouse was Sharkey's 'brother from another mother'.

Late on Friday afternoon, all the puppies and Sharkey were given a skills test, and, as each passed the week's lessons, they were awarded a bright blue flea collar. To Xander's amusement, Duchess even secured one on Sharkey. Knowing that she considered a collar equivalent to leg irons or a ball and chain, Xander expected a strong negative response and was surprised when Sharkey's reaction was a blushing nose and a big smile. "What's with you?" he asked, when he got the chance. "I thought you hated collars."

Sharkey's nose turned a deeper crimson. "I learned they could be an award for achievement, not just a symbol of slavery."

"Good for you," he said, proud to know she was open minded enough to weigh the value of new information. "Tomorrow morning, I plan to return to Port Antonio."

"So soon?"

He nodded. "I need to finish my survey before June, because that is when the storms usually start."

"So, you'll be leaving Jamaica completely."

"Yes. Hurricanes and tropical storms can wreak havoc. That plus the high percentage of dogs and the political instability of many of these island countries makes it important to have safe places."

"And you're responsible for that." It wasn't a question, but he nodded anyway. "Will you ever come back?"

"When I can, but I don't know when that might be. Simon seems to be capable of handling things." Xander hoped his confidence wasn't misplaced. "And if he needs help, I'm sure Dame Esmeralda would advise him."

"Probably Duke and Duchess, too."

He didn't doubt that for a minute, though he would never say so out loud. While he no longer viewed each and every dog as a demon, he still believed that either due to heredity or environment, a significant portion of the species qualified.

"I'll miss you," Sharkey admitted to her toes.

"I've enjoyed your company, too." He glanced around the compound. "Will you stay here and continue to attend class?"

"I think so." Her attention remained fixed on her toes.

"Good." Her head popped up in surprise. "Since you'll be

here, you'll be able to keep me posted on this training operation." He smiled. "Something tells me that you'll be more objective than some of the others, who only see what they want to see."

"I can try, but I don't know how to contact you."

"That's easy."

Soon, he and Dame Esmeralda were instructing her on the use of computers and the codes, which kittens usually mastered in their first month of life.

When they finished, Dame Esmeralda took Xander on a stroll around the grounds, "I'm thrilled with Sharkey's decision to stay."

"I figured you would be, but why do you seem surprised?"

"I assumed that she would return to Port Antonio. That is her home, after all."

"I'm not sure she has ever had much of a home. Besides, I'll be sailing back to the Bahamas, as soon as possible." He batted away a buzzing insect. "It is her life and her choice, but if I had anything to say about it, I would think it would probably be better for her to be here, with friends."

"Did she tell you that Mouse will be heading back with you?"

"No. Are you sure she knows?"

She thought for a moment, then shrugged. "Perhaps not."

As she had considered her answer to his question, he had realized that she intended him to travel across half the island with a puppy. "I really don't need an escort."

"But he might."

"I beg your pardon?" Xander asked, now quite confused by the conversation. Had she just said that she wanted him to play bodyguard for a puppy? The thought was so disorienting that he nearly sat down.

"Mouse volunteered to infiltrate the dog training camp you reported about."

"The one in the mangroves?"

She nodded. "Since both of you seem to be heading for the same general area, it seems sensible for you to travel together."

"True," he agreed, even though every emotion he had warred with her indisputable logic.

"Excellent," she purred. "You will leave in the morning, after we break the night's fast."

"So you have this all planned."

"Indeed." She swished her elegant tail and proceeded along the path with majestic dignity. "The gardener is being dispatched to the Port Antonio market to buy pork and some other things Cook needs, so he will be driving withing a few blocks of their training facility."

Meowser! It sounded like she was talking about door to door limo-service for a trek that had taken him and Sharkey more than two harrowing days of bug bites, singed paws, humiliating bathes and that revolting landing in rotting fish entrails. He inclined his head with the proper dignity, "I appreciate you organizing this," he said.

Chapter 14

The following morning, Sharkey stared at him and Mouse in shock. "You're going where?" Her voice was shrill. "To do what?"

"Infiltrate the training facility in the mangroves," Mouse calmly repeated.

"And you didn't think it was important to mention that to me until now?"

Mouse dipped his head. "I thought it was of primary importance not to mention my mission to you until the last moment."

Sharkey sputtered with so much rage that for a minute, not a single intelligible sound came out. Then, she whirled toward Xander. "You taught me that power and rank are nice, but true friends are more important." He nodded. "And you think this is how a friend should treat someone they say is their BFF?"

Dame Esmeralda stepped between them. "You may not agree. Actually, at this exact moment, I know you will not agree, but accepting this is the best way you can prove your friendship with Mouse." Sharky vibrated with so much rage that all her hair stood on end and her back arched. Esmeralda ignored her battle-ready body language and continued to speak calmly. "The mission

Mouse volunteered for is dangerous and our information says that there is a strong anti-cat mentality there. How well do you think he would do if you were living in the area and the friendship you shared became known?" She cocked an ear and some of the starch seemed to go out of Sharky's fur. "This will be our very first mission of this sort and it is crucial to give it the best possible chance of success. Besides, it is not going to last forever, merely four months, to determine if it will work."

"Four months is forever," Sharky muttered, but her body-language proclaimed that she was starting to accept it.

Simon, Mouse and Xander arrived in Port Antonio before noon. Simon and Xander spent several hours watching the training facility's activity from the boughs of a well-placed Flame of the Forest tree, while Mouse napped on the ground. For the first time in his life, Xander thought that dogs' inability to climb a tree was a disadvantage because Mouse was unable to utilize vantage-point.

One thing Xander had not counted on was the fact that his humans had moved Whispurring Winds off the dock and his home was now anchored near C Pause, in the harbor. He wasn't sure if he was more annoyed about the fact that they had moved his home without his approval or if he was primarily annoyed at the challenge of getting home without getting wet.

Shortly after twilight, Mouse said, "It's time." But instead of marching the block downhill to the veiled entrance of the facility, he continued to sit, unmoving except for chewing his lower lip. Xander realized that the puppy must be afraid to move forward on his mission

Xander tilted his head. "Do I need to push you?"

"No," Mouse sighed, as if accepting the inevitable. "You

need to come down here and hit me and Simon needs to do that limb-walk thing to get to a safer place."

"Beg pardon?"

"You heard me." Mouse's eyes narrowed. "Did you think I could just walk down there stinking of cat and get a good welcome?" He woofed in disgust.

"Cats do not stink," Simon said.

"You say that because you can't smell your own stench, yet I bet you can smell dogs." Mouse snorted in disgust. "Well, guess what, you cats smell as bad to us as we do to you."

"I doubt that, but I will not sit here and debate the issue. Now that the sun is down, it's time for me to head to the bus station." Simon tilted his ear in the direction of the market. "Riding on top of a bus is best done at night."

Xander nodded. "If I'd known the schedule, that would have been my first choice." And a lot better than landing in rotten fish-guts.

"Don't doubt that cats stink. Believe it. I have always been straight with you." Mouse glared up the tree. "Simon, please move along. Once this begins, there will be a lot of dogs down here and believe me, you don't want to be noticed or have your movements watched."

"He's probably correct," Xander said. "This is his mission and getting back to the survey is mine... You need to get back to Kingston." Xander batted an ear at an unseen biting bug.

"Good," Mouse said, "then we're all agreed on who needs to do what, so get your tail down here and hit me."

Fine. The boy wanted him to punch him, he would.

Xander quickly climbed down the trunk and aimed a halfhearted swipe at Mouse's big pointy ear, but the pup easily avoided it.

"That was pitiful. Even worse than that so-called demo we gave the babies." Mouse snorted.

"What?" Xander snarled.

"Oh, please, do you expect me to believe the Great Kamikaze can't fight better than a month-old puppy?"

"I didn't want to hurt you."

Mouse laughed. "More like you didn't want to show how a real fighter moves."

"Maybe that, too." Xander studied Mouse, and realized that the pup figured the best first impression he could make in order to be accepted by the mangrove dogs was to be involved in a cat fight. 'Look, I really don't want to hurt you. This mission is important to Dame Esmeralda and-"

"Do not tell me some self-righteous blather. I thought this through before I volunteered and this is my best bet. Yeah, I might get hurt, but so might you. Is that what you're afraid of?"

"Are you trying to make me angry?"

"Is it working?"

"Not really."

"Then perhaps this will get you in the mood." With a lightening quick move, Mouse pounced on him and, if not for his extensive training, nearly managed to sink his teeth in his neck. Xander managed to leap backward, just in time.

Mouse spat out some fur.

Xander's training kicked in and, with a war whoop, he whirled free of the sharp teeth, continued the turn and kicked Mouse in the side.

The puppy yelped in pain as he fell, but by the time Xander had his paws centered, Mouse was in a fighting stance.

A flock of parakeets, that had been settling into the boughs of a nearby tree took off in panicked flight.

Mouse growled and lunged.

Xander easily sidestepped, noting the puppy was favoring its left side. Good, the kick had done its intended damage. Xander faked to his left, then kicked the already injured side.

Mouse howled with pain.

Distant howls answered.

"Is this what you wanted?" Xander asked.

"Yes," Mouse said, as he lunged forward, his teeth missing Xander's ear by a breath.

Xander used the puppy's own momentum and flipped him, so he summersaulted away. Meanwhile, Xander moved so he was in position to get a glimpse of the gap in the mangroves, from which dogs were streaming.

"You got your audience. Better make it look good."

Mouse lunged at him.

Xander screamed in pain and terror, even though the painful bite got no closer than the one before. In another moment, the dogs would be upon him. "Later." With a leap, he vaulted a patch of mint, then quickly climbed the flame of the forest tree he had previously used as a lookout post, scooted around the trunk and moved into a convenient breadfruit tree.

Once on the far side of that tree, where he could not be seen by the pack, he again moved out onto a branch, which intersected with the branch of another flame tree. By the time the pack was howling at the base of the first tree, Xander was four trees away.

Still, he kept to the shadows, and looked before he moved.

The ignorant dogs formed a circle around the tree trunk and howled.

Satisfied that their attention was in the wrong direction and that Mouse seemed to have achieved instant acceptance, Xander turned his attention to the dilemma of getting home and staying dry. He spotted a board lying on the shore, which looked like it was the right size to use to surf, then saw a large red plastic bag, which the wind had apparently blown against a bush with big pink flowers. Good, there was a strong breeze from the right direction. Plan made, he quickly climbed down the far side of the rough-barked tree he was in, and made a beeline across the road toward the beach.

When the dogs' wailing didn't change in pitch, he knew his seal-point coat had, again, masked his movements. Xander grabbed the plastic bag, then with a bound, landed on the board with enough force to send it careening into the bay.

Grasping the bag the way Merlin had taught him, Xander held it into the breeze and sailed the plank close to Whispurring Winds.

He dropped the bag on the still floating board, then leaped aboard the stern and headed toward the bow to watch the dogs, who were still screaming for him to come down from the tree. Whiskers twirling with delight, he watched the pack howl at he base of the flame of the forest tree, where they were ignorant enough to believe he was trapped.

As he rounded the cabin, he spotted Valentine on C Pause's front deck, his attention on the pack. Xander made a big production of stretching, as he hailed the boxer, "What's going on with your friends?"

Valentine jumped, and collided with a black plastic bag, which was, again, lashed to the front deck. "What are you doing there?"

"Aside from having a good nap ruined?" Xander doubted the dog could see the bits of dust and bark on his fur in the increasing dusk.

"You left days ago."

"Yep."

"When did you get back?"

"A while ago."

"What'd you do? Swim?"

"Do I look wet?"

Valentine frowned as he peered across the water. "Where's your girlfriend?"

Xander shrugged. "She was just a girl, not my girlfriend." He pointed an ear toward the howling pack. "You're the one with the girls after him. So, how come you aren't over there with them? It sounds like they've treed a raccoon or something. I thought you liked that sort of thing."

Valentine shook his head so hard that globs of slobber big enough to be seen in the waining light that dotted C Pause's untidy deck.

Xander was glad their boats were no longer tied together. The mutt was a cleaning challenge. "And how come all the trash is tied on your deck, again?"

"What?" He tapped the closest black bag. "This?" Xander nodded. Valentine woofed. "These are medical supplies and an operating tent."

"Huh. Looks like trash to me. Your deck looks better without that junk there."

"How'd you know it was gone while you were gone?"

Xander snorted. "Just because I've been straying out of sight does not mean I can't look out a porthole and keep track of things." Pretending ignorance, he asked, "How come you need that stuff?"

"Not your business, Valentine growled.

"Fine." The moon began to rise. "Well, I'll talk to you later." Trying to appear casual, Xander walked back to the cockpit, then headed into the salon.

Since his humans were not aboard, Xander had plenty of time to download all the information he had collected in his collar's data base, then file his reports. He concluded his report on Dame Esmeralda by typing, 'Though change can be difficult, life is about change. Sir Simon's alliance with the mongoose and herons allows him many options, which help him succeed. This all leads to new formal alliance for running Jamaica, which should equalize our ability to gain crucial information and avoid conflict.'

While he was not ready to include any positive comments about the potential of some dogs as allies in an official report, he intended to keep an open mind and see how Mouse progressed.

THE END

About Jeanne Foguth

Though Jeanne began her career technical writing, her love of romantic-suspense, whether it be present, future or in an unknown galaxy inspired her to write the novels she wanted to find in bookstores. Since marrying, Jeanne and her husband have lived from the arctic to the tropics, as well as from yacht to off-grid mountain home. She loves using vivid colors and flowing shapes in her oil paintings as well as creating edible landscapes. She recently finished preparing previously-published novels for their digital debut, and is now working on new stories.

You can always find out what she is working on and/or contact her at:

Her blog:

http://foguth.wordpress.com

Her web-home:

http://www.jeannefoguth.com/

OR Facebook:

https://www.facebook.com/jeannefoguth

Other books by Jeanne Foguth

Contemporary Suspense/Romance

Deadly Rumors (for adults; all other titles = 13+)

Fatal Attractions

Passion's Fire

Purrtector Series, a Feline Fantasy staring Xander de Hunter

The Red Claw

Purr-a-noia (Coming in Summer of2015)

Chatterre Trilogy (Kazza's sci/fantasy Trilogy)

Star Bridge

Thunder Moon (Coming in Spring of2015)

Fire Island (Coming in Winter of 2015)